THE TILTING HOUSE

THE TILTING HOUSE

BY TOM LLEWELLYN

ILLUSTRATIONS BY SARAH WATTS

TRICYCLE PRESS

Berkeley

Tricycle Press and the Tricycle Press colophon are registered trademarks of
Random House, Inc.

Library of Congress Cataloging-in-Publication Data

Llewellyn, Tom (Thomas Richard), 1964-
   The tilting house / by Tom Llewellyn ; [illustrations by Sarah Watts]. — 1st ed.
   p. cm.
   Summary: When Josh, his parents, grandfather, and eight-year-old brother move into
the old Tilton House, they discover such strange things as talking rats, a dimmer switch
that makes the house invisible, and a powder that makes objects grow.
   [1. Dwellings—Fiction. 2. Eccentrics and eccentricities—Fiction. 3. Family life—
Washington (State)—Fiction. 4. Rats—Fiction. 5. Human-animal relationships—
Fiction. 6. Washington (State)—Fiction.] I. Watts, Sarah (Sarah Lynn), 1986- ill.
II. Title.
   PZ7.L7724Til 2010
   [Fic]—dc22
                              2009049275

ISBN 978-1-58246-288-2 (hardcover)
ISBN 978-1-58246-350-6 (Gibraltar lib. bdg.)

Printed in U.S.A.

Design by Betsy Stromberg
Typeset in Cartographers Wheel, Fournier, Grant Rustic Opti, and Tree Persimmon
The illustrations in this book were drawn in pen and ink, scanned, and then colored
and textured digitally.

1 2 3 4 5 6 — 14 13 12 11 10

First Edition

JLG   1600   10/10

THIS ONE'S FOR DEB.

CONTENTS

THREE DEGREES AT 1418

THE WOODEN SIGN on the porch read TILTON HOUSE.

"Why's it called that?" I asked. No one knew. Not even the real estate agent, Mrs. Fleming—though the way her hands were shaking made me wonder if she was hiding something.

We were all standing in the house's front yard next to an overgrown holly tree that reached higher than the rooftop.

"Fourteen eighteen North Holly Street," said Mom, looking over the information sheet. "This is the cheapest house in the neighborhood, even though it's got to be one of the biggest." Mom looked up at the agent. "What's the deal?"

"Maybe we should go inside before I answer that," said Mrs. Fleming. "The previous owner was a bit eccentric."

"It's a classic," said Dad. "Looks like a custom design. It's got a nice big front porch, and it's in a decent neighborhood."

My little brother, Aaron, and I glanced at the house next door when Dad said this. Boards covered most of its windows.

The house in front of us wasn't in much better shape. The two windows on the second floor and the sloping roof over the porch made me think of a gray old man with a drooping mustache.

Half an hour earlier, I would have said that any house was better than the cramped apartments we'd called home my whole life. Now I wasn't so sure.

"It needs paint," Mom pointed out.

"So we can paint it," said Dad. "What's your favorite color? Josh and Aaron'll help—won't you, boys?"

"Can we paint it today?" asked Aaron.

"See?" said Dad. "The boys are excited."

"I'm not," I said. "This place looks like a dump."

"Quiet, Josh," Dad said quickly.

"You'd only be the second owner," Mrs. Fleming chimed in. "The original owner lived here more than seventy-five years."

"Oh, is he . . . ?"

Mrs. Fleming nodded. "Yes. He passed away just recently."

"A dead guy lived here?" Aaron asked me in a whisper.

"Before he was dead," I replied. "Not after."

"Oh. Good."

"Who's that man across the street?" asked Mom. "He's staring at us." On the front steps of the well-kept old home opposite sat an elderly man. He was looking right at us and his lips were moving, but from where we stood we couldn't hear what he was saying.

"I'm sure he's harmless, honey," said Dad. "Anyway, you're the one who's always saying you're sick of living in apartments. This is our chance! There is no way we could afford another house like this."

"Well, let's look inside," said Mom. "But there's got to be a reason it's so cheap."

We followed Mrs. Fleming up the front steps. She unlocked the door and placed a shaky hand on the doorknob. Then she hesitated and turned to face us.

"Now, it may be a bit . . . unnerving when you go inside, but remember what a good price this is. And remember what wonders a coat of paint can do." She smiled weakly and opened the door.

We walked inside and the world tipped.

Aaron fell against me.

"Watch it!" I said.

"I can't help it!"

Mrs. Fleming sighed. "The floor tilts three degrees precisely. If you're thinking the house is settling, it's not. It's as solid as a rock. The house was built this way and I can show you the original blueprints to prove it."

"You mean the whole house is like this?" asked Mom.

"I'm afraid it is. Every room."

"Why would someone design a house with tilting floors?"

"I don't know," said Mrs. Fleming, checking her watch. "It's a bit of a mystery."

"Cool!" said Aaron. I glared at him and took a few steps into the hall.

A ray of sunshine streamed through the open doorway, lighting up swirling particles of dust. As my eyes adjusted to the dimness, I noticed something. Words, numbers, diagrams, and drawings scribbled in pen and pencil covered the walls, the railings, and most of the floor.

"Walls are easy to paint," Mrs. Fleming said, following my gaze.

"I wouldn't dream of painting it," said Dad softly. He walked lopsidedly to the nearest wall. On the faded rose-patterned wallpaper, the words *quadratic ionization*, were written in spidery script next to a drawing of a cone-shaped device. Wires connected the cone to the ears of a beautifully drawn and detailed human head. A chart of numbers next to the head was labeled *amplified bioacoustics*.

"It's strangely beautiful," Dad said. "Honey, this could be an important work of outsider art. The museum should know about it." He turned back to Mrs. Flemming. "Was the owner an artist?"

"I don't know. None of the neighbors ever met him."

"I thought you said he died just recently."

"He kept to himself," said Mrs. Fleming. "That's what the neighbors say at least. But neighbors say a lot of things." Her hands were shaking harder than ever. "I can drop an additional ten thousand off the price if you make an offer today."

"No one *ever* met him?" I asked.

"I'm sure someone did." She put her hands behind her back. "Look, I understand if you're not interested. I've shown this house over twenty times and no one's ever gone past the entry. Just say the word and we can go our separate ways. No hard feelings."

"I never said we didn't want it," said Dad. He turned to Mom, who was shaking her head. "Give it a chance, hon. This house could be a serious artistic find. Look at the detail on these drawings."

"They look like they were drawn by a crazy man," Mom said.

4

"People thought Van Gogh was a crazy man." Dad was trying to win her over—Van Gogh was Mom's favorite artist. "And look at the trim! It's probably cherry."

"Actually, it's holly," said Mrs. Fleming.

"Did you hear that? Holly! Holly trim on Holly Street. What other house has holly trim? Look at the carving on this stairway. And what about these original wood floors?"

"I saw them. They're all tilting."

"Okay!" cried Mrs. Fleming. "I'll drop the price by twenty thousand, but that's as low as I can go!"

"It's not low enough," I piped in.

"Josh!"

We bought the house. For that price, Mom said she could get used to the tilt and the scribbles. I think she realized that Dad was right: We'd never be able to afford a house half as big on Dad's art museum salary and the money Mom made working part time at the school office. We were doomed to live in a dumpy, tilting house.

Two weeks later, on the first day of summer vacation, we moved in: Mom, Dad, Grandpa, my brother, Aaron, our cat, Molly, and me. We left behind a two-bedroom apartment across town, where my parents had one bedroom, Aaron and Grandpa the other, and where I had slept on the living room couch.

On moving day, while the rest of us hefted boxes, Grandpa eased into the porch swing and pulled out his pipe and tobacco pouch. His wooden leg made him kind of wobbly, so he sat puffing and directing traffic.

Aaron and I stopped a moment to rest on the porch. Grandpa ran his hand along the carved armrest of the swing. "This is fine craftsmanship. Some of the best I've seen. I can tell that this porch swing and I are gonna be good friends," he said. "Now I can smoke even when it's raining."

He leaned back and then pointed his pipe stem at the man across the street—the same old man we'd seen before. "Interesting gentleman over there," said Grandpa. "He's been sitting jabbering to himself for the last half hour."

Later that afternoon, after we'd unloaded most of the boxes, Mom dragged Aaron and me over to say hello to our new neighbor. He looked even older than Grandpa. His white hair was combed straight back. His face was deeply wrinkled, and thick eyebrows nearly hid his eyes. Weirdly enough, though, his clothes looked freshly ironed.

The man didn't look up when we got to his porch. He just kept muttering to himself.

"Maybe he's hard of hearing," said Aaron. "HELLO! WE'RE YOUR NEW NEIGHBORS!" The Talker—that's what we later named him—continued to stare straight ahead at our house.

"She may have been the rawest and most unlettered of the talking picture stars," he mumbled. "The entire contents of the box had escaped. Only one thing remained." Then he said something about a place called St. Hubert and "a dead Belgian with staring eyes." Mom pushed us along as we walked quickly back across the street.

Immediately to the south of our new house sat a duplex. There were two mailboxes and two front doors—one leading to the upstairs apartment and the other to the downstairs one. Nobody lived in either. The grass needed mowing.

To the north sat the house with the boarded windows. Faded sky blue paint was peeling off its remaining shingles. A purple front door was buried behind wagon wheels, stuffed animals, old mailboxes, and a huge set of deer antlers. The grass needed mowing there, too.

The man who lived in the house with the purple door had a mop of greasy gray hair and wore flip-flops, shorts, and an unbuttoned Hawaiian shirt. He glared at Aaron and me on moving day when we said hi to him.

"Keep it down."

"Keep what down?" I asked.

"The noise."

All the other houses on our block had fresh paint and neat yards, and the neighborhood overall seemed pretty normal.

But the only other kid our age who lived on Holly Street told me it wasn't. Her name was Lola. She lived in the green house on the corner with her mom and stepdad. She was a year younger than me, but taller by at least three inches.

"It's definitely not normal around here," she said, twirling a strand of curly dark hair. "And you're living in the weirdest house of all. Everyone says so. The tilting floors are just the beginning."

"What do you mean?" I may have agreed that our new house was weird, but I didn't like her saying so.

She shook her head. All she would say was, "No one's seen the guy who lived there for sixty years. And my stepdad says you have rats."

Lola was right. We found the rats the very next day. The day somebody died in our new house with the tilting floors. Somebody named Jimmy.

THE ALL-THE-WAY-UP ROOM

MOM HAD HOPED that Dad would change his mind and paint over the walls before we moved in. I'd hoped so, too. There was no way I was going to invite friends over to this place with the walls looking like that. But they remained covered in cryptic writing as we unpacked boxes in the kitchen. "I'm not going to be happy if I have to live with all these scribbles," said Mom.

"Don't think of them as scribbles, honey. Think of them as art," said Dad. "The man was probably a crazy genius!"

"You need to take down that wallpaper, Hal."

"First I have to schedule a professional photo shoot. It's my responsibility as an art curator."

9

"When is that going to happen?"

"I'll put it on my to-do list."

That afternoon, Dad took a break from arranging and unloading and found Aaron and me in the living room where we were shelving books. Dad plunked down on the couch, and his body leaned to the right. He wiped the sweat off his forehead and let out a sigh. "Guess I'm gonna have to prop up all the furniture."

I stared at the words on the wall behind his head:

Invisibility, electricity, and the refractive index of air.

It didn't look like art to me. It looked like something I was supposed to have learned in school.

"Whaddya say you boys and me take five and poke around a bit?"

"Poke around where?" I asked.

"Around our new house. I'll bet if we look in every nook and cranny, we'll uncover a secret or two."

"A secret?" asked Aaron. "What kind of secret?"

"I don't know." Dad grinned as he struggled to get up from the tilting couch. "A house built with tilting floors has got to have secrets."

"It's got to have a screw loose," I said.

"Smart aleck."

We started in the garage and found a dusty clock tucked away on a corner shelf. We wiped it off and brought it inside to see if it worked.

"Too bad we don't have a fireplace," said Dad. "We could set this on the mantel."

"I'm glad we don't have one," said Aaron.

"Why?"

"Because the floors tilt. I might fall into the fire."

Dad said we needed to find a level surface to test the clock. "It's not going to be easy in this house," he said, clearing a moving box off the dining room table and setting the clock down. He started the pendulum swinging, and the clock ticked happily away.

"Hal," said Grandpa from the other end of the table, where he'd been working on a crossword, "it appears you set that clock down on the one thing in this house that's not tilting."

The dining room set had come with the house. Dad figured it had belonged to the previous owner.

"Why doesn't the table tilt?" asked Dad, leaning down and looking at the legs.

"Don't you see? The table and chairs were custom made for this house. Look, the legs at that end are longer than the legs at this end. Whoever made them did some excellent work." Grandpa patted the smooth surface of the table.

"It's a long shot, but I'll bet. . . ." Grandpa slipped out of his seat and examined the underside of the table. "I knew it! Look at this, boys!"

We all crouched under the table. "See this name carved here?"

"Who's 'Lennis'?" Dad asked.

Grandpa gave Dad a sour look and pulled himself back into his chair. He rolled up the pant leg to reveal his wooden leg. "This," he said, "is Lennis. Or I should say, Lennis is the name of the old codger who carved this stump. Best carpenter I ever met. Must've made this dining room set, too."

"You think this table's worth something?"

"Only to someone with tilting floors."

11

"We've got plenty of those," I said.

Dad wanted to look in the crawl space under the house, so Aaron and I followed him outside to a three-foot-high door under the back porch. We unlatched it and looked inside. Spiderwebs stretched across the doorway, with nothing beyond but darkness.

"No way am I going in there," I said. "You go, Dad."

"I bet no one's been down here in fifty years. Maybe we can find out why this house was built with tilting floors."

"Close the door," said Aaron. "I don't like it."

"Me neither. Can we just finish unpacking?" I asked. I could feel goose bumps on my arms and legs.

"Aww, come on, you scaredy-cats," said Dad. "This is uncharted territory." He ducked and found a light switch. A yellow bulb cast shadows across the crawl space. Dad hunched inside, batting cobwebs as he went. Aaron and I stood in the doorway, as still as stones.

"Nothing but dirt," Dad called back to us. The cobwebs frosting his hair made him look old, like Grandpa.

We went back into the house. In the second-floor bathroom we found a cupboard next to the toilet. Mom came in with a box of cleaning supplies and asked Aaron and me to put them in there. While Dad continued searching the house, we hurried to fill the cupboard with scrub brushes, spray bottles, and rolls of paper towels. We slammed the door and heard a scream from the floor below.

Aaron and I ran downstairs to find Mom standing in the laundry room, rubbing her head gingerly. Paper towels and bottles of cleaner lay scattered at her feet. We all looked up and saw an open trapdoor in the ceiling.

I ran back upstairs and opened the cupboard. It was empty now.

"Heads up!" I yelled and tossed a pink washcloth in the cupboard. I closed the door, then opened it. The washcloth was gone. When I raced downstairs again, the cloth was resting crookedly on top of Mom's head.

"It's a laundry chute," Mom said. "When you close the door up there, this one down here opens and drops everything on my head. So please stop."

Back in the bathroom, we found words and numbers scratched into the mirror above the sink. When I looked at my reflection, I could see two words right above my face.

"*Rattus rattus,*" I whispered. Aaron began chanting the words over and over.

"*Rattus! Rattus!*"

"Quiet!" I yelled. Below my chin were the words "Biological, acoustical information transfer. Sound and meaning. Tongue clicks vs. squeaks." None of it made any sense.

"*Rattus! Rattus!*" shouted Aaron, pulling me away from the mirror and across the hall to our room.

I'd argued briefly for my own room, but Aaron had looked so worried about sleeping alone that I gave in without much of a fight. At least I wasn't on the living room couch—and now I had a door that closed, a real bed, and walls for hanging posters.

Drawings of prickly leaves, little round berries, and squatty trees covered the walls of our bedroom. They were holly trees, just like the ones growing outside. The words *ilex aquifolium* were scrawled everywhere, along with sketches of seeds and cutaway diagrams of tree trunks. We were going to need a lot of posters.

A coworker of Dad's had given us an old set of bunk beds, and Mom had leveled them on the tilting floor by stacking books under one end. Now they were level but wobbly. Aaron climbed up to his top bunk and began rocking the beds back and forth. *"Rattus! Rattus!* I got the top bunk and you got the bottom. *Rattus! Rattus!"* shouted Aaron.

"Would you knock it off and come on up here!" called Dad from somewhere above us. "I think I found something!" We followed his voice to the master bedroom where a door opened to a steep stairway that led to the third floor—or the All-the-Way-Up Room, as Aaron had already named it.

The floors up there tilted toward the center just like everywhere else. The walls were covered in even more scribbles, so crammed together that they were nearly impossible to read. Dad stood at the far end of the room next to a panel built into the wall—it was the same size as the door to the crawl space.

"What do you think is in there, boys?"

I shrugged. Aaron looked worried. Dad dropped to his knees and pushed on the panel. We heard a click and the panel swung outward.

"I guess it's the attic," said Dad. "I wonder how big it is." He stuck his head inside. "It's dark, but it looks like it's full of boxes!" He began to feel around. "I can't find a light switch."

Suddenly, he screamed and jerked his head out of the doorway. Something furry clung to the top of his head. Dad slapped at it, but whatever it was had its claws buried in Dad's hair. Finally, he grabbed it, then let out another scream. "Aaauugghh! It bit me!" He threw the little animal to the floor and brought his shoe down on it, hard. I heard a tiny crack, like the sound of a potato chip breaking. Then the animal lay still.

Aaron and I stared at it. Dad breathed heavily. "I think it's a rat. Just a baby," he said, with a half laugh. "No big deal. Probably just wandered in from outside. No need to tell your mom."

"But you hurt him," Aaron said, his voice breaking. "You killed him. You killed the baby rattus!" Aaron cried until his shoulders shook. Dad hugged him, but Aaron kept crying and repeating, "You killed the baby rattus!"

When Aaron finally calmed down, the room grew quiet. That's when we heard someone else crying—a soft, uneven sound.

"It sounds like it's coming from the attic," I said, pointing to the door. We all looked at one another.

"Come on," Dad said. "Let's find a flashlight." After a few minutes of unsuccessfully searching for a working flashlight, we returned with a lamp and an extension cord.

The body of the baby rat had disappeared.

"I guess he wasn't dead after all," Dad said. Aaron gave a hopeful sniff.

Dad plugged in the lamp, clicked it on, and set it inside the dark attic. We peeked inside. The space stretched on past the glow of the light, making it hard to tell how big the attic was. It smelled like a wet dog that had rolled in dead fish. Old boxes lay scattered under the low, slanted ceiling. The lid on the nearest one sat askew. The crying seemed to be coming from there. Dad pulled back the lid.

Eight pairs of tiny, shining black eyes stared up at us. The eyes belonged to a family of rats huddled around the limp body of the one Dad had killed. All the faces staring up at us looked frightened. All except one. The biggest rat looked mad. He stood on his back legs, stared right at us, and threw his front paws up in the air.

"You got a lot of nerve!" the rat yelled. "It ain't enough that you murder my son, but now you interrupt us during our moment of grief! You got no decency!"

The rat scurried up the side of the cardboard box, jumped out, and darted over to Dad's feet. He sat up on his hind legs and thrust out his big, hairless belly. "You're a bum!" he shouted at Dad. "You're a murdering bum and I want you outta here!" We backed out of the dark room, the rat marching after us. He kept yelling. "You bust into my home. You kill my kid in cold blood. You don't deserve to live!"

The rat followed us into the room and closed the panel door after him, groaning and straining against its weight, but when Dad tried to help, the rat waved him away angrily. He turned again to face us. "I ain't through talking to you," he said to Dad, "but I don't want the missus or the kids to hear what I'm gonna say. They been through enough already, what with you smashing my Jimmy."

"He bit me!" Dad said. "I'll probably have to get rabies shots!"

"Rabies?!" said the rat. "You really are a jerk, you know that? You saying my kids are vermin? When your kids bite some other snot-nosed human kids, do they spread rabies? Would you kill them, too?"

"N-n-no," stumbled Dad, "but they're not rats."

"No, they ain't rats. They sure ain't rats. Neither are you. A rat would never do the rotten thing you did. If your sons were rats, they wouldn't have to worry about their old man going around smashing helpless little kids. 'Cause that's what you did. You smashed a helpless kid. You killed my son. My Jimmy. My Jim. You're gonna pay for what you done. You're gonna make it right." Then he burst into tears.

That's the part of the whole thing I remember most. The part when the tough-looking rat sobbed uncontrollably and Dad stood there, trying to figure out what to say. Dad told me later it struck him right then what it would feel like to have one of us die.

"Mr. Rat," he said softly, "what would you like me to do?"

The rat straightened out his whiskers, sniffed a few times, and said, "Well, now. The first thing you gotta do is get outta this house."

"What?" Dad cried. "That's crazy. I just borrowed three years' worth of wages for this place. I'm not about to leave. I may be willing to try to make things right, Mr. Rat, but let's be reasonable."

"Reasonable!" the rat yelled. "Be reasonable with a murdering fink like you? This is my home and I want you out!"

"Your home? What's your home? The cardboard box?"

"Box? No, I ain't talkin' about that stinkin' box!"

"Well, what, then? This attic? Do you want this entire attic? Because—"

"What, are you nuts? An attic ain't a home! An attic is a room in a home!"

"Then what do you mean? What's your home?"

"This—this whole place!" The rat waved his paws around. "This whole house! The upstairs and down and the attic, too. The kitchen, the living room, the dining room. All the bedrooms and all the stinking bathrooms. The front yard, the backyard, the driveway, and the pile of junk behind the garage. That's my junk." His voice grew calm, and he stared into Dad's eyes. "This whole rotten house is our home. It was my great-great-great-grandfather who first moved in here when Tilton was alive. It's what we're accustomed to. You just got here. Thanks for stopping by and killing my son. Now it's time for you—and your rotten kids—to go."

I thought the rat was right, but I kept my mouth shut.

Dad was silent a moment. Then he rubbed his eyes with the palms of his hands and said carefully, "We're not going to leave, Mr. Rat—"

17

"Mr. Daga. Would you stop callin' me Mr. Rat? My name is John Daga, but you're gonna call me *Mister* Daga. And who are you?"

"You can call me Hal, Mr. Daga. Hal Peshik. These are my sons, Josh and Aaron."

"Josh and Aaron, eh? A little advice, young Peshiks: Don't turn out like your dad, because he's a murderin' fink."

"No, I'm not! Look, I'll give you the attic for a couple of weeks," said Dad, "until you can find a new home for your family. But that's it."

"That ain't gonna cut it, Peshik," said Mr. Daga. "No bum is gonna force us to live in an attic."

"You're rats," Dad said, firmly. "If you haven't noticed, you're forcible." He turned and guided my brother and me down the stairs. Before we shut the door to the All-the-Way-Up Room, we heard Mr. Daga shout after us: "You're gonna pay for what you've done, Peshik. I'm gonna see to that."

MR. DAGA

LOOKING BACK, I guess we should have expected what happened that night.

About an hour after dinner, we were watching TV in the living room when the power went out. No more lights and no more TV. I followed Dad out the back door to the breaker box. A minuscule note was stuck to the panel door with something sticky and smelly. Three words were written in tiny, shaky letters:

Time to pay.

"'Time to pay,'" mumbled Dad. "Fine. We'll see who's going to pay."

Mom was standing at the back door. "Pay what? What's going on, Hal?"

"Nothing," Dad said. "It's just a little, er, mouse."

"You're going to pay a mouse?"

"Or maybe a rat."

"A rat? I hate rats!"

"I know. I know. And this one talks. His name is Mr. Daga."

"Cute," said Mom, with a smirk. "Could you please just get the electricity turned back on? And if there are really rats in this house, Hal—"

"Don't worry. I've got it covered." Dad marched up the stairs. Aaron and I jogged to keep up. In the All-the-Way-Up Room, Dad popped open the secret attic door. The box still sat there, but the Daga family had left only a few tattered pieces of fabric.

"We'll call an electrician in the morning," said Dad. "It's summertime. We can live without lights for a little while."

"What about TV?" said Aaron.

"We can live without TV, too!" yelled Dad. He marched out to the garage, where the electricity still worked, and ran an orange extension cord all the way into the kitchen so we could plug in the fridge. The refrigerator started humming again, but if you asked me, it sounded kind of nervous.

That night, I dreamed that talking rats were crawling around under my blankets. Aaron woke me up when he yelled at me to stop rocking the bed.

The next morning, as I sat drinking some orange juice in the kitchen, Mom opened the cereal cupboard and let out a scream.

"Rat droppings! There are rat droppings in my kitchen!"

I looked over her shoulder. Little black crumbs lay scattered all around the cereal boxes.

We skipped breakfast that morning.

After an expensive visit from the electrician, the lights finally came back on. The electrician said it looked like something had chewed through our wires, and recommended we call an exterminator. Dad nodded, but he never made the call. I was glad he didn't. Even if Mr. Daga was making life tough for us, I didn't want him dead.

Aaron switched on the television set in the living room and settled on the couch. Mom went into the laundry room to do a load of laundry. I followed Dad upstairs to see if the rats had returned to the attic.

When we walked by the upstairs bathroom, a horrible smell came from it. The cupboard next to the toilet was open and a pile of rat droppings lay inside.

"Oh, goodness," said Dad. "Don't let your mom see that."

"See what?" came Mom's voice from the laundry room downstairs.

Startled, Dad slammed the cupboard door shut. As the scream came from below, we realized he had just emptied a laundry chute full of rat droppings onto Mom's head.

The power went off again halfway through Mom's shower. She had to finish in the dark.

"Maybe we can watch TV at that girl Lola's place," said Aaron.

"No way," I said, recalling Lola's comments about our house. "She's mean."

The next day, tiny holes started appearing in Dad's favorite shirts. Mom refused to open any of the cupboards for fear she might find more rat droppings. She would have. The black crumbs were in every corner of the house. And she banned Aaron and me

21

from the attic. "I don't ever want you boys going up there!" she yelled. "A rat might bite you. You might get rabies."

"Mr. Daga said he doesn't have rabies," said Aaron.

"Who is Mr. Daga?"

"The talking rat."

"Very funny. A comedian, just like your father."

Molly, our cat, wasn't much help. Molly was so old that she was more like a striped orange beanbag than a cat. She was definitely too old to catch anything.

Dad and I were brushing our teeth in the bathroom one morning when we heard a voice as if from nowhere.

"You ready to pay for what you've done, Peshik?"

"Where are you?" Dad said, looking around.

"I'm up in the bathroom fan."

"Oh, yes. I can smell you now," said Dad, crinkling his nose.

"Watch it, wise guy," said Mr. Daga. He burped. "Ooh! Sorry. Had an old hotdog for breakfast. Anyway, I figure it's safe up here, since you ain't had no electricity for the last week and a half." He laughed.

"Thanks to you," said Dad. "And now my wife won't go near the kitchen because of all the rat droppings."

"Quit your whining, Peshik," said Mr. Daga. "You humans sure have a problem with poop. Rats don't mind a bit of poop. Heck, we poop in our own nests. As for your lights, they'll come back on as soon as you settle."

"What do you want from us?" Dad asked.

"We want a home of our own. We want security from all you stinking humans. We'd prefer to stay in this house since we've been here so long, but we're willin' to relocate if necessary."

"Dear Lord," mumbled Dad. "How in the world could I ever

afford another house? I'm an art museum employee! Do you realize how little I get paid?"

"Tell you what, Peshik," said Mr. Daga. "I'll help you with the money. Who knows? You might even come out ahead on the deal, 'cause I've got a pretty valuable collection of stuff. Us rats are real good at finding things. Expensive things."

Dad shook his head and went back to brushing his teeth. He spit, rinsed, and said, "So what you're saying is, you'll help pay for a house with little things you and your children have found?"

"Now you're getting it," said Mr. Daga, sounding pleased. "Hey, you wait right there and I'll give you a sample." We heard the scurrying of tiny feet, then silence.

Dad and I looked at each other, not knowing what to expect. A minute later the scurrying feet returned. "Heads up!" called Mr. Daga. A silver coin dropped out of the vent and fell to the bathroom floor. Dad picked it up.

"It's a dime," he said with a shrug. "It's gonna take a lot of dimes to buy a house."

"For a guy who works in a museum, you don't know much about old stuff, do ya?" asked Mr. Daga. "It ain't just a dime, smart boy. It's an 1897 Barber dime. A gem-brilliant proof. Accordin' to the book, only seven hundred and thirty-one proofs were struck. You should be able to get at least fifteen hundred bucks for it at a decent coin shop, if ya got any brains at all. Try it. I'll check back with you tomorrow."

I took a look at the coin. On one side, it had a face that looked like Julius Caesar's. On the other, there was a wreath made out of wheat.

After we finished getting dressed, Dad found a coin shop in the Tacoma phone book.

"Where are you going?" asked Mom as we headed for the front door. She was sitting at the kitchen table, having a cup of tea with Grandpa.

"To a coin shop. Mr. Daga gave us a rare coin he wants us to get appraised."

"Mr. Daga? The rat?"

"Yes, dear."

"And he collects coins?"

"Apparently so."

"If you get his coins appraised, will he stop pooping in my cupboards?"

"It's complicated."

We were walking out to the car when Dad stopped and stared at the duplex next door.

"What?" I asked.

"Place has been vacant awhile," he said, nodding in its direction. Then, without saying another word, he got in the car and we drove to the coin shop.

When we showed him the dime, the man behind the counter gave a low whistle. Then he looked in a book and went to the back room to make a phone call. When he came out, he told us he would pay $1,450 for it.

The next morning, Mr. Daga spoke to us again through the bathroom fan vent. "So? What'd ya find?" he asked.

"You were right," said Dad. "How many of those do you have?"

"That's the only 1897 Barber dime," said Mr. Daga, "but I got an 1857 S Double Eagle twenty-dollar gold piece. It's worth about ten grand, accordin' to the book. It's the pride of the Daga collection. We got a whole bunch of coins, includin' some—"

"Wait!" Dad said. "I have an idea!" He ran from the room. By the time I said goodbye to Mr. Daga and went downstairs, Dad had left. He came back home around lunchtime, rattled off something to Mom about the electricity coming back on soon, and ran upstairs to the bathroom. I arrived behind him in time to see him yelling up to the vent.

"Mr. Daga! I've got news for you. I think I found a house for your family!" We heard those tiny feet and smelled that rat smell.

"Tell me the news," said Mr. Daga. He sounded excited.

"Well," said Dad, still trying to catch his breath, "it's the duplex next door. Since it's a duplex, it has room for two families, but the owner hasn't managed to rent either the upstairs or the downstairs for about a year and a half. I talked to him. He said he's losing money on it every month and is willing to sell the whole thing for a good price."

"A duplex, huh?" asked Mr. Daga.

"Yes. You could live in the top floor and rent out the bottom, if you wanted. It's next door, which would make relocating much easier. I would help you buy it with the proceeds from the sale of your collection. If you rented out the bottom floor, you'd have income for paying taxes, insurance, and other upkeep costs."

"Yeah, a little extra dough would be okay. And it might be handy to have humans around, so long as they stayed downstairs. And didn't kill us or nothin'."

"They would. Stay downstairs, I mean."

"Humans mean food. Cereal. And hotdogs. I hope they like hotdogs. So you'd help us buy this house, right, Peshik?"

"I would."

"When can I see it?"

"The owner said we could look at it anytime."

"How about now?"

"I can't do it now. I'm on my lunch break. My boss, Mr. Stevens, will throw a fit if I'm back late."

"Sounds like a swell guy."

"You have no idea."

"How about tomorrow? Say eight A.M.?"

"Eight A.M. it is. Now how about fixing our electricity?" But all we heard were his tiny, scratching footsteps.

The next morning at eight, Mr. Daga stood waiting for us on the bathroom counter, leaning against the cold water knob with his tail curled around his feet. I had forgotten how bright his eyes shone and how bad he smelled up close. On the mirror I saw the words *rattus rattus* again above his reflection. They read like a caption.

"Since yer so stinking big," Mr. Daga said to Dad, "I'll let you carry me in your shirt pocket." Dad nodded and held out his hand. Mr. Daga climbed on easily. He jumped into Dad's pocket, rearranged himself, and poked his nose and eyes out. His whiskers twitched left, then right. "This'll work," he said. "Move it."

At the end of the tour, Mr. Daga said he thought the duplex would be "an okay joint, with a little work." Over the next few days, he and Dad made numerous trips to the coin collector in town, as well as to one in Seattle, with Mr. Daga hiding in Dad's shirt pocket. By the end of the week, they'd managed to collect just enough money to buy the house.

That night, right as I climbed into bed, all the lights came on. "Hallelujah," Mom shouted from downstairs.

Dad, Aaron, and I helped the Daga family move the next day. Grandpa said he wanted no part in dealing with rats, so he stayed home.

I had no idea rats kept so many things. Most of their belongings looked like garbage to me—bunches of seeds and wads of toilet paper and stashes of rotten food. Some things made no sense, like a sandwich bag stuffed with bird bones and feathers. Some were beautiful: tiny polished stones; old photographs of people who looked like my Grandpa, with the corners of the photos rounded off by tiny teeth; bits of metal and glass. I asked if there were any more coins, but Mr. Daga said they'd been forced to sell every last piece of the collection to purchase the duplex. "Nothing left of the collection but pennies. I miss the other coins a little," he said. "They were nice to look at and touch, but that kind of thing ain't worth much to a rat. That's human stuff."

The last thing we moved was a bundle about three inches long, wrapped carefully in a piece of old corduroy that had disappeared from Mom's sewing drawer. Mr. Daga told Dad it would be good for his soul if he'd carry it to their new home, explaining that it was the body of Jimmy, the young rat Dad had killed with his shoe. I stood back, watching the quiet faces of the rat family, thinking how I would feel if that were my little brother's body.

Dad set the bundle in a corner of the new living room, as instructed. Mr. Daga quietly explained that rat custom was to leave the body of a loved one wrapped in cloth until the flesh had completely decomposed and the bones lay clean and white.

Once everything was moved in, the young rats ran around the duplex, exploring every nook and cranny of the rooms. Mr. Daga looked like a proud homeowner, sharpening his whiskers with his tiny claws, slapping his belly, and breathing in the air of his new home as if it smelled better than the air in our house. It did—it wasn't covered in rat droppings. At least not yet.

The upstairs unit of the duplex still looked empty by human standards: no chairs, no couches—just a few cardboard boxes here and there and mounds of paper shavings in the corners. The counters stood empty. The mantel over the fireplace was dusty but uncluttered.

That mantel caught Dad's attention. "Do me a favor, Josh," he said to me, and then whispered instructions in my ear. I nodded and ran home. When I came back, Dad met me at the door and carried the mantel clock into the Dagas' new living room.

"I think this would look good in your home," he said, setting the gift on the mantel.

"Tilton's old clock," Mr. Daga said. "Nice touch, Peshik. You sure you want to give that away?"

"We have no fireplace and no mantel," Dad explained. "And you do. Besides, you should have a housewarming gift."

"Thanks," said Mr. Daga. "I like it real good. Someday maybe I'll show you how it works." I wondered what he meant by that. It would be more than a year before I found out.

"Do you think you'll be happy here?" asked Dad.

"I think so," Mr. Daga said. "I'm almost sure of it. Heck, you might even end up thinkin' I'm an okay neighbor. After all, I know even more about yer house than you do."

"I believe it." Dad smiled.

Mr. Daga smiled back. "You should. Remember, no one knows a house like a rat knows a house. Oh, and if you ever have trouble with your electricity, just let me know."

THE VULTURES

THANKS TO GRANDPA, it wasn't long before the Dagas had rented the bottom floor of their duplex. A broken hip had recently forced Grandpa's old fishing buddy Mr. Natalie into a wheelchair, so he and his wife had been looking for a house with all the rooms on one floor.

On the day the Natalies moved in, Grandpa settled himself onto our porch swing like before, smoking his pipe. Aaron and I sat next to him, waiting for the moving truck to arrive. Mom had told the Natalies that we'd help them with the boxes. The three of us stared across the street at the Talker, who was chattering away to no one in particular. "Sometime I'm gonna sit down next to that man and just listen to him go," Grandpa said. "Why, for all we know, he's reciting the cure for cancer."

"Dad says he's crazy as a loon."

"Watch it there, Josh. One of these days your dad's gonna start talking that way about me."

The moving truck turned onto our street and before long Aaron, Dad, and I were lugging boxes. Mom was inside helping Mrs. Natalie unpack. I decided I really liked Mrs. Natalie, because she kept telling us what a good job we were doing and how strong we were, and she gave us pop to drink. I didn't like Nat, as Grandpa called Mr. Natalie, because he yelled at us to stay out of his way. Nat was so fat that he filled his wheelchair side to side and front to back and even spilled over a little. He wore a captain's hat pulled low over his eyes, and he smoked a pipe like Grandpa. He made a bubbly sound when he talked, as if his mouth were full of spit. I'd heard dozens of stories about Nat from Grandpa—how he'd loved hiking through the woods and fly-fishing in the middle of a river. Looking at him now, it seemed impossible this could be the same guy.

After moving day, we saw Mr. Natalie only when he drove his motorized wheelchair down the porch ramp and around the block. He never said a word, but we could hear the whine of the chair's motor and see the smoke from his pipe billowing out behind him. He looked like a tugboat. Dad said he always wanted to tell Mr. Natalie that his engine was burning a little oil. Grandpa assured him Nat would not appreciate the joke.

The front yard of the duplex gave Mrs. Natalie space to grow her beloved azaleas. "I am a gardener," she told Aaron and me one morning, "and I'm going to spend my remaining days transforming this little piece of brown earth into a green paradise. If you boys would like to earn some extra money, I could use your help. I pay three dollars an hour for good work and four dollars an hour for great work."

We weeded and planted for her two mornings a week for the rest of the summer. I never did get more than three dollars an hour from her.

It was on the third of those mornings that I first saw the black Cadillac.

We saw fancy cars in our neighborhood sometimes, so I didn't pay much attention until the Cadillac stopped in front of the Natalies' house. Even then, Mrs. Natalie stayed on her knees, weeding away. The Cadillac doors opened and two men climbed out: one tall and thin, the other short. They wore matching black suits and narrow black ties. The tall one hunched his shoulders and jutted his chin out, which made him look like a perching crow. The short one shuffled along after him, twitching his ridiculously bushy mustache. They stepped up to Mrs. Natalie's fence. "Good day, young gentlemen, madam." The tall, thin one nodded in turn at Aaron and me, then at Mrs. Natalie. "Is this the home of . . . ahhh—" He turned to his companion. "Give me the list, Ludwig."

"I don't have it. I gave it to you on our last call and you never gave it back."

The other man began to panic. "I certainly did give it back! Check your other pockets, you fool! We've only got the one copy!" He pulled out a hanky and mopped his forehead. I set down my trowel and watched as the short, chubby man called Ludwig ran his hands through all his pockets. He finally yanked out a long roll of yellowed paper. Both men sighed. The tall man snatched the list from Ludwig, gave his forehead one final mop, and carefully tucked his hanky back into his pocket. He took a deep breath and smiled at Mrs. Natalie.

"I'm nothing without my list. You could say we live and die by the list. Please be more careful, Ludwig. Now then, where were we?" He ran a long, thin finger down the names. "Yes, here it is: Natalie, John. Is this the home of John Natalie?" Mrs. Natalie stood up, removed her gloves, and said it was.

The man smiled toothily. "My name is Peat. Victor Peat. I believe I represent products and services of interest to you. Let me give you my card."

Mrs. Natalie took the card and read it out loud: "Victor Peat, Complete Funeral Arrangements." She tried handing the card back with a simple "No thank you."

Victor Peat made no move to retrieve his card. "Let me leave you a few of our catalogs. You know, we have a complete line of coffins, from the sublimely elegant to the surprisingly economical. We also offer headstones, burial plots, complete funeral services, hearse rentals, and other related products."

"Fine," said Mrs. Natalie, "but none of that is of interest to me. Nobody's dead."

Victor Peat smiled again. "Of course not. But please take this information and put it someplace handy. If we ever can be of service, just call. Number's on the card."

"Fine," repeated Mrs. Natalie impatiently. She took the catalogs and watched as Victor Peat and his assistant walked back to their Cadillac.

"Put the list in your inside coat pocket, like I told you," said Victor Peat. Ludwig obeyed. They climbed in the car and drove slowly away.

That night, John Natalie died of a heart attack. He was seventy-two years old and at least sixty pounds overweight.

Two days later, I saw the black Cadillac again. It drove past our house and parked in front of the duplex. I watched through the front window as Victor Peat and Ludwig climbed up the stairs. Mrs. Natalie met them at the gate and invited them inside.

Our family went to the funeral. A lot of people Grandpa's age attended. They all seemed to know Grandpa from way back and kept calling him Red—Mom said that Grandpa's hair was red before it went gray. I couldn't remember ever seeing Grandpa—even in a photograph—with anything other than his thin silvery hair.

A lot of those old people had interesting stories to tell about Nat, the fat, grumpy old man I'd only known for a few weeks. Considering how little I liked the guy, I was surprised by how much I didn't hate his funeral. Victor Peat and Ludwig made sure everything ran smoothly. The punch tasted especially good. It had orange sherbet in it.

I didn't think about that black Cadillac or Victor Peat until two weeks later, when I saw the car parked in front of Lola's house. The day before, her stepdad, Jerry, had died of a burst appendix. I wasn't about to go to Lola's to ask her about the car, since every time I saw her on the street, she made fun of our tilting floors or asked if I'd seen any rats in our house. In fact, I probably wouldn't have said anything at all if Lola hadn't said something first.

We saw her at her stepdad's funeral. The service had ended and a couple of women who looked like old versions of Lola were serving refreshments in the reception area of the funeral home. My brother and I were scooping that same orange sherbet punch into our glasses when Lola walked up.

"What are you two doing here?"

"We came with our parents." No one spoke for a while, because what do you say at a funeral?

"That guy gives me the creeps," said Lola, finally.

"What guy?"

"That guy. Mr. Peat." She pointed across the room at Victor Peat, who was standing next to Lola's mom. He was smiling, jutting his chin in her direction.

"He's the same guy who arranged Mr. Natalie's funeral," I said.

"He's creepy. He came by our house and tried to sell us a coffin. Then Jerry died the very next day, out of the blue. It gives me the shivers just thinking about it."

"He came by Mr. Natalie's house the day before he died, too," I whispered. "We were there, helping Mrs. Natalie weed the garden. He gave her a catalog of coffins and gravestones."

"He did?" asked Lola. "That's so creepy." Then one of her relatives called her away.

"Do you think maybe he had something to do with it?" Aaron asked.

"Something to do with what?"

"With them dying."

"I don't know. I don't see how he could have. They died in different ways. It's not like they were murdered or anything. But it's like he *knew* they were going to die. When he came to the Natalies', he had Mr. Natalie's name on a list."

"Vultures," said Aaron.

"What?"

"They're like vultures. Like those birds that circle over dying cows."

The next time I saw Victor Peat was early on a Saturday morning. Dad is a pancake fanatic and usually makes a big breakfast on Saturday. It was seven thirty and Grandpa, Aaron, and I were sitting at the kitchen table while Dad mixed ingredients. Mom was still in bed. Dad tried to let her sleep in each Saturday, but

Aaron usually ended up waking her early to ask her where his shoes were or what we'd be having for lunch later.

We were going to start painting the outside of the house that day, and Dad had forced Aaron and me to go to bed early the night before. When someone knocked on the door, it was so early that we assumed it was somebody we knew. Aaron yelled, "COME IN!"

"Shush," Dad hissed. "Mom's still asleep." No one came in.

I raced Aaron to the door and won. I pulled the door open as Aaron stampeded down the hallway, while Dad shushed us again from the kitchen. Aaron stopped dead when he saw Victor Peat.

"Good morning," Mr. Peat said, smiling thinly. "I'm sorry to bother you so early, but I'm looking for the home of a young man named . . ." Ludwig handed him the list. "Ah! A young man named Aaron Peshik. Would one of you be Aaron Peshik?"

I looked over at my brother. His face was turning white.

"Who is it?" hissed Dad from the kitchen. "Tell 'em to come in!"

Victor Peat removed his hat and stepped past us into the kitchen. Ludwig followed him, scanning the writing on our walls without comment. Aaron stared after Victor Peat, his eyes filling with tears and his lips quivering.

"Don't worry, Aaron," I said. "It doesn't mean anything. He's just some freaky guy. Don't worry about it, okay?"

Aaron burst out crying and collapsed onto the floor. Who could blame him? Wherever this weird guy went, people died the next day.

Dad came in from the kitchen. "Josh, could you see what's wrong with your brother?" He apologized to Victor Peat and Ludwig, then ushered them out the front door, saying he wasn't interested in their services.

"Please take this information and put it someplace handy," Victor Peat said, stepping over a sobbing Aaron. "If ever we can be of assistance, just call. Number's on the card."

Dad nodded and accepted a stack of papers. Victor Peat reached a bony hand down to Aaron and patted him on the head. "Don't worry, young man. Whatever's troubling you now will soon be a distant memory."

Aaron cried even louder as Dad closed the front door. Dad knelt down and tried to comfort Aaron, but when Aaron starts crying like that, it's impossible to talk to him. Dad turned to me for help.

"It's that guy, Dad. Victor Peat."

"Victor Peat?" He looked down at the card in his hand and frowned. "How'd you know his name?"

"He's the same guy who planned the funerals for Mr. Natalie and Jerry."

"Oh, right," said Dad. "That's where I've seen him."

"And both times he showed up the day before those guys died and tried to sell them coffins."

"He's a vulture!" blubbered Aaron. "And he said he was looking for me!"

I think Dad understood how scary it would be, especially for a little kid like Aaron, but he didn't believe there was any connection. He tried to comfort Aaron by tickling him and finally offering him candy. None of it worked, so he picked Aaron up, set him on the couch with the Saturday comics, and went to clean the breakfast dishes.

As soon as he left the room, Aaron whimpered, "I'm gonna die!"

I had to agree. Aaron was going to die.

I helped Dad in the kitchen, and then we went outside and started covering the bushes with drop cloths. Thinking about Mr. Peat's visit distracted me so much that I kept fumbling with the corners and turning the cloths the wrong way. I could tell that Dad was trying hard not to yell at me.

We found a wooden ladder in the side yard. All the rungs tilted, so we knew it must have belonged to the original owner. It made it a little tricky for Dad to stand on.

"Hold the ladder steady!" Dad yelled from the top rung. He began to roll the first coat of gray-blue paint over the wall of the house. I could almost swear that Tilton House shivered with pleasure. I was surprised at how beautiful the color looked, and suddenly I really wanted to see what the house would look like when Dad was done.

But I knew I couldn't spend all morning helping Dad. There was no way to know how much time we had before the vultures claimed their victim. Somehow, I had to find a way to save Aaron. I was so preoccupied that it took me a moment to realize the ladder was tipping. I grabbed it tightly and barely managed to keep Dad from crashing to the ground. "Josh!" yelled Dad. "Please be more careful!"

Please be more careful. Hadn't Victor Peat said the same thing at Mrs. Natalie's front gate? I thought of what else he'd said that day: "I'm nothing without my list. You could say we live and die by the list." A desperate, crazy idea formed in my head. I let go of the ladder and ran to the front door.

"Josh! Where are you going?" Dad yelled after me. I didn't answer. I found Aaron still curled up on the couch.

"Let's go see Lola," I said.

"Why?"

"I think we can beat Victor Peat and his list. But we've got to ask Lola a question first."

A minute later, Aaron and I were knocking on Lola's front door for the first time ever. She looked surprised to see us.

"What do you want?"

"Can we talk to you?"

She stepped back wordlessly and we walked in. I knew our house seemed weird to her—even though she'd never been inside it. But her house—with its complete lack of dust and clutter—seemed weird to me. Someone had polished the bare—level—wood floors in the entryway to a high shine. By contrast, our entryway was always a tilting jumble of shoes, Frisbees, and skateboards. The furniture in Lola's house, what little there was, looked brand new and uncomfortable. I stood up straighter and wanted to tuck in my T-shirt.

"We can go up to my room," she said. We followed her upstairs. The door to her room had a brass plaque on it that read DOLORES'S ROOM.

"Who's Dolores?" I asked.

"I am."

"I thought your name was Lola."

"Dolores is my full name. Only my mom calls me that, so don't even think about it."

"We wanted to ask you about your stepdad."

She opened the door. Her room didn't look like it was part of the same house. The floor was buried in stuffed animals, CD cases, books, soccer trophies, stacks of drawings, and polished rocks. Aaron picked up a very round, black rock and turned it slowly in his hand.

"My stepdad's dead," said Lola.

"I know. I'm sorry. But Mr. Peat just came to our house this morning and he was looking for Aaron." I explained to Lola about the visit and our theory about the list.

Lola sat down on top of a stuffed elephant on her bed. She stared at me. "I've seen the list. Mr. Peat had Jerry's name on it the day before he died."

"That proves it!" I said. "We need to get that list."

"I'm dead! I'm dead!" cried Aaron.

"Shut up," said Lola, but even Lola couldn't keep Aaron from sobbing. Lola pulled him in front of her. She cupped his face in her hands and stared directly into his eyes. "Look at me," she said, surprisingly gently. "We're going to get that list. If we can destroy it, you won't die. But you've got to stop crying, okay?"

Aaron sobbed away.

"If you stop, I'll let you keep that rock your holding."

Aaron looked down at the rock and sniffled loudly.

"Good job. Now you and Josh get your bikes. I'll meet you in front of my house in five minutes."

I had to admit, when it came to blubbering little kids, Lola was pretty good.

We rode our bikes to the address on Victor Peat's business card—the same funeral home we'd been to twice before. There was a sign out front: PEAT AND PEAT. COMPLETE FUNERAL ARRANGEMENTS.

The lobby had dark carpeting, straight-backed chairs, and a black coffeepot oozing steam. I asked a frizzy-haired woman sitting at a desk if Victor Peat was there. She told us he and Ludwig were out calling on prospective clients.

"They'll be back this evening at five o'clock for a funeral but won't be available to meet with anyone until Monday morning. Is there something I can help you with?"

I mumbled, "No thanks," and we went outside.

"What are we going to do?" asked Aaron. "If we don't get the list before Monday, I'll be dead."

"We go home for now," Lola said. "And we come back here at five o'clock, for the funeral. That's our only hope."

When we got home, Dad was still painting. He'd made remarkable progress on the front of the house, tilted ladder and all. I told him I'd felt sorry for Aaron and had thought of a way to cheer him up. Dad still yelled at me, so I took my position at the bottom of the ladder again. I stayed there, helping him move the ladder, until four o'clock.

At four thirty, Aaron and I were in our bedroom, putting on our dressiest clothes—black pants, white shirts, and clip-on ties. Aaron looked horrible. He'd been crying all day and his whole face was puffy and red. At a quarter to five, Aaron and I were sneaking out the back door when we heard Mom call us to set the table for dinner. We made a run for it. Aaron's life was on the line. We had no choice.

Lola met us in front of her house. She was wearing a dress and looked years older than me. We pedaled hard until we reached the chapel, where we hid our bikes in the bushes out front and went inside.

The chapel was crowded, so we sat in the back row. A minister told us all about a man named Joe Lampkin. According to the minister, Joe had worked as a garbage collector, always remembered his nephews' birthdays, and was a friend to everyone on his route. Between frightened sniffs, Aaron said the dead man sounded like a nice guy.

"Everyone sounds nice at their funeral," said Lola. "That's the rule."

In a few minutes, Victor and Ludwig Peat entered the chapel through a side door. They watched the rest of the service quietly, and then Victor Peat went to the front of the chapel and invited all the guests to the reception area, where they could "enjoy some refreshments and reminisce with friends and loved ones."

"Ludwig keeps the list in his inside coat pocket," I whispered to Aaron and Lola. "If we can get him to take off his coat, we can snatch it and get rid of it when we're safe at home."

"How do we get him to take his coat off?" Aaron asked.

"I don't know. Let's go to the fellowship room and see what we can figure out."

When we entered the reception area, Aaron grabbed my arm and pointed to the punch bowl. "We could get punch and spill it on Ludwig's jacket. He'd take it off if it was wet." Lola and I followed him over and watched him fill a glass.

"It's too small," Lola said. "Spill that on him and he'll just wipe his jacket with a napkin. We need a bigger glass."

"No, we don't," said Aaron. "We just need more of them."

He filled three more glasses and barely managed to pick all four up at once. With four full glasses balanced in his stubby hands, Aaron was ready, but when we looked around for Victor Peat and Ludwig, they were nowhere to be seen.

"You've got to find them!" hissed Aaron. "I can't carry these cups around all night! I'm about to drop them as it is."

"Follow me," Lola whispered back. We left the reception area and went into the chapel. All the chairs were empty now. Even Joe Lampkin had been wheeled out. We went upstairs to the office, but it was empty, too. Back downstairs, I looked out the front door and saw the tall, thin man and the short, chubby man walking casually down the sidewalk toward their black Cadillac.

"Mr. Peat!" I yelled out the door. "Wait!" Both men turned around. We walked quickly to them.

"How can I help you?" said Mr. Peat, politely.

Aaron answered by running up to Ludwig and throwing all four glasses of punch at his chest.

"What are you doing?" Ludwig yelled. "You little brat! You've ruined my suit!" He began to remove the drenched jacket, but Victor Peat stopped him.

"Don't you see what's going on here?" said Mr. Peat, his voice low and menacing. "We buried this girl's stepfather not long ago. And we saw these two boys on our first visit this morning. This young one is Aaron Peshik. His name is on the list."

"The list?" said Ludwig. "Oh, I see. It's the list you're after. Trying to steal it, are you? Destroy the list and save yourselves? It's been tried before, you know."

"Give it to me," said Victor Peat.

Ludwig reached inside his sopping wet jacket and pulled the roll of yellow paper from his pocket. Victor Peat snatched it from him and shrieked.

"It's ruined!"

Punch and ink dripped from the list. From where I was standing, the names looked completely illegible.

Victor Peat frantically unrolled the paper, spreading it out on the hood of the car. It was nothing but a smeared, soggy sheet. He turned and faced us.

"Well, young man," he said to Aaron, "it appears you've succeeded. Your name is no longer on the list. I do not know what will happen to you now. You might live forever. Now scat!"

We scatted. We grabbed our bikes and pedaled home as fast as we could. We were riding so fast, we didn't slow down for the busy intersection at Eleventh Street. We didn't see the brown pickup truck barreling toward us. The driver laid on his horn, slammed on his brakes, spun sideways, and slid right at us. We slammed on our brakes, too. I braced myself for the crash.

The truck stopped two inches from Aaron. The driver yanked open the door.

"You kids okay?"

"Yeah."

"You need to be more careful. You could have been killed."

"We know," Aaron said. "Sorry."

We pedaled slowly the rest of the way. Aaron thanked Lola for her help. "You're welcome," she said, before riding off toward her house. When we opened the back door, Mom and Dad were waiting for us. They were already mad that we'd run off without saying anything, so we didn't tell them about Aaron's near miss with the pickup truck. By the time they'd finished yelling at us and hugging us, they'd also forbidden us from riding our bikes for two weeks.

GRANDPA'S WOODEN LEG

"I DON'T FEEL SO GOOD," I said the morning after the incident with Mr. Peat.

"You don't look so good, either," said Mom. She placed her hand on my cheek and frowned. She set me on the couch and snuggled a blanket around me, which I didn't mind. When Mom left the room, I told Aaron I'd probably gotten sick from all the stress of the day before. He shrugged.

"I feel great," he said. "I'm gonna go get some cereal. You want anything?"

Mom and Dad let Aaron stay home from church with Grandpa and me. Aaron and I sat on the couch watching TV all morning.

I nodded in and out of sleep while Aaron swung his feet and sang along with the theme songs. The couch was level now, like nearly all of the furniture in our house. We'd stuck books under the legs at one end, and as long as you sat still, the books stayed in place.

After lunch, Grandpa limped in and stood in front of the set, blocking our view. "Still not feeling well, eh, kid?" I shook my head. "Seems to me you need a good story to cheer you up. Did I ever tell you how I ended up with this here wooden stump?"

"Yes," said Aaron, "but tell it again."

"Wasn't talking to you. Talking to sicko, here."

It was Sunday afternoon, which, according to Grandpa, was the part of the week set aside by God Himself for smoking, swapping stories, and taking naps. He shut off the TV and sat himself down in the green chair he'd brought with him when he moved in with us years ago. He pulled out his pipe and began stuffing it with tobacco.

"Are you going to smoke that in here?" I asked.

"You think anyone'd notice?" Grandpa said, looking up at me from beneath his bushy gray eyebrows. "Oh, I guess I'd better not, but it's awful hard for me to tell a story without a pipe to smoke." He settled back into his seat. "Well now, I been thinking about this ol' story for a few weeks now, what with Nat's passing and all. Good man, Nat, but it was his fault I traded in my pink flesh for this here chunk of maple." Grandpa rapped on his wooden leg with his pipe. "Was his fishing hook that caused all the trouble.

"It was back when your dad was just born, when I was sharing that little one-bedroom house over in Milton with a baby and your grandma. Needless to say, I was always on the lookout for an excuse to go fishin'. Anyways, it was round about June and we were having a real warm year, so I called Nat and asked if maybe him and me could head out to the Dosewallips and try our luck with the brook trout that had escaped us thus far."

"Were you both serious fisherman?" I asked.

"Oh, Nat was. I've never been all that interested in catching fish. All a fish on your line means is that you have to wake up from a perfectly good nap. So we went to our favorite spot, near Brinnon, just as the sun was coming up. I set up under this old cedar tree that had roots growing into the water. Right off the bat, Nat sees a fish jump, so he drops his tackle box, pulls on his waders, and he's off. Me, I kinda lean back, stick a few salmon eggs on my hook, and cast it out into the water. Next thing I know, I'm snoring away.

"I wake up in an hour or so and it's already hot in the sunshine, so I kick my shoes off and dangle my toes in the water. I can see Nat down about a hundred yards, and he's like a war general executing his attack. My backside's about numb by this time, so I stand up to stretch. Sure enough, my bare right foot lands on a fish hook. It'd spilled out when Nat dropped his tackle box. It jabs right into the fleshy part of my heel. I pull it out of my heel, barb and all, along with a chunk of my foot the size of a raisin. Hurt like the blazes, and blood is dripping into the water. So I stick my foot back in the river and pretty soon it's feeling better and I forget about it. At the end of the day, I pull on my socks and shoes and we head back home. "

"Did you catch any fish?" asked Aaron.

"Fish? Come to think of it, I did all right. Just sitting there on the bank, I caught one less trout than Nat that day, and my biggest was bigger than his biggest. I brought 'em home to your grandma, hoping she'd clean 'em for me, but she was too busy with the baby. So I did it myself and fed the innards to the cats.

"A few days later, my foot started to hurt. I didn't think much of it that first day. But when I woke up the following morning, it was hurting all the way up to my knee and I could feel my heart beating in my heel.

"'What'd you do to yourself this time?' your grandma asked me. I said I didn't do nothing except step on a little old fishhook. She makes me peel off my sock and takes a look. Well, my foot is swollen tight. The bottom of it is as red as the devil himself, and there's this black line working its way up my leg.

"When she sees that black line, your grandma nearly faints dead away. She gets on the phone quick and before I know it she's driving me over to the doctor's office. Same drill there: I peel off my sock and Dr. Bruell takes a look and lets out a low whistle. 'Is it bad?' I ask him. 'It's not good,' he says. "Blood poisoning." He makes a phone call and tells me we need to head over to the hospital in Tacoma. 'Today?' I ask him. 'Right now,' he says. So your grandma, Dr. Bruell, and I head on over there. A couple of other doctors take a look. They step outside to talk, and then Dr. Bruell and this tall German doctor come back in. Grandma's standing up and Dr. Bruell asks her to sit down.

"'Red,' the doc says to me, 'the leg's got to go. You've got blood poisoning, and if we wait any longer, it'll spread up to your heart and you'll be dead. If we amputate now, we'll only have to take the leg from the knee down.'

"Well now, news like that can shake a fella. Grandma's crying away, asking if there's anything else they can do, but I knew the doc was givin' it to me straight and there was no use arguing, so I told him to take it quick. Next thing I know, I'm in an operating room and they're strapping a mask over my nose and mouth and then I'm asleep.

"When I wake, I don't feel anything, which is good, because during my nap the doctors had taken a saw and cut off a good chunk of my leg: bone, meat, and all. I'm so doped up that I can barely remember where I am. Then I do remember and I try to sit upright. I finally manage to reach to where my leg should be, but below the knee, there's nothing there. All that's left is a big stump of white bandages soaked red with so much blood that I can smell the iron.

"Once the dope wore off it hurt like the dickens. It felt like my whole body was on fire. Let me tell you, boys, I was ready to go down to hell to cool off—that's how hot it burned. They couldn't give me enough dope to make it stop hurting.

"I was in the hospital for about two more weeks, and then I finally got to go back home. I'd sit in a chair and stare at the wall and yell for your grandma to bring me things. I about drove her to the nuthouse.

"I finally got so I could hobble around on crutches, and I made it back to the shop, where I could get along all right if I was sittin' down. After work, I'd sit in my chair in the living room and growl at your grandma and at your dad, who was just a little baby who hadn't done a thing wrong—leastways not that I knew about.

"Finally your grandma couldn't take any more of it, so she calls Dr. Bruell and he shows up one day for a surprise visit. He asks how I'm doing and I ask him how he thinks I'm doing, what with my leg cut off and all. He says he'd like us to go for a little drive, because there's a guy he wants me to meet. I cuss back that if I want to go for a drive I'm still capable of driving myself just fine. Our Olds was an automatic, see, and it only takes one foot to operate an automatic, since there ain't no clutch pedal to push. So Dr. Bruell, he says fine, I can do the driving and he'll give me the directions.

"So we climb into the Olds and we drive all the way up Meridian Street to the town of Graham, where this friend of his lives. We pull up and I see it's a furniture shop: Lennis and Company."

"Lennis? That's who made our dining room set!" said Aaron.

"Right. The porch swing, too, I bet. Anyway, we walk into the barn and there's Lennis all covered in sawdust, working at a wood lathe, sawdust sticking to the sweat all over his bald head. He brushes off enough of the dust to shake hands with the doc and asks how the doc's new kitchen cabinets are working out. Dr. Bruell tells him they're wonderful, but that he wants to talk about a different kind of project. He goes on to tell Lennis my story and asks him if he can make me a wooden leg.

"Now, I'm not sure if I'm keen on the idea, but neither one of them seems to care much what I think. Old Lennis, he stares me up and down. He measures all over my good leg with complicated metal calipers, and he makes all sorts of notes in his little notebook. Then he rolls up my pants and takes a look at my stump. Asks me a few questions about where it hurts. He asks if he can take a look at my remaining foot. He draws a bunch of pictures of it and measures each toe with tiny little clamps and tapes and pieces of string. Dr. Bruell gives him one of my old right shoes, which he had brought along without telling me. Lennis says, 'Got a nice piece of kiln-dried maple. Was going to turn it into a pedestal for a kitchen table, but it might work all right for this, too. Gimme a couple of weeks.'

"Sure enough, two weeks later, there's a knock on the door and Lennis is standing there holding my wooden leg. This same one here. Same leather pad on top. Same straps. Same rusty metal hinge for the knee. Said he made the hinge out of an old saw blade. Carved the ankle and the toes and even carved in the toenails.

See? Took me a while to figure out how to use it without falling over, and I still hobble around like a three-legged dog, but ol' Lennis and me, we do okay together. Heck, if I can walk around in this dad-blamed funhouse we all live in now, then I guess I got no right to complain."

Grandpa looked down forlornly at his unlit pipe. He stood up and headed for the front porch. "In a funny way, you might say this ol' leg has come home. To this house, where it has the company of the dining room set. This leg and that dining set are brothers, come from the same maker."

"Is that a true story?" Aaron asked.

"You insult me, boy," said Grandpa, striking a match as he reached the front door. "Course it's true. Ain't interesting enough to be a lie. Now hush up and let your brother get himself some rest."

THE ATTIG

THE NEXT MORNING I broke out with red bumps around my armpits and behind my ears. Mom took me to see Dr. Trumble, who diagnosed me with Teufelskreis measles. The doctor ordered Aaron, Dad, and Grandpa to stay out of the house for two weeks, so they moved in with our friends the Mullens, who lived across town. Mom could stay, because she'd had Teufelskreis measles when she was a little girl. Dad came by Tilton House after work to keep painting the exteriors, but he wasn't allowed to come inside.

I hated living away from Aaron that long. Aaron drove me crazy sometimes, but I missed him. While Aaron got to live at the

53

Mullens' house, with level floors and a hot tub in the backyard, I had to stay among the mad drawings and the tilting floors.

The Teufelskreis measles made me miserable for the first three days. My eyes glazed over, my lips puffed up, and my joints swelled until I could no longer bend at the waist. It took a while, but the swelling and the red bumps slowly went away. After a week I felt fine and was more than ready to play outside.

"Not a chance," said Mom. "You're contagious. And you could relapse, so you're stuck in here with me for another whole week."

Besides Molly the cat, the only living thing I saw in fourteen days was Mom. I played all the board games, read all the books, watched all the TV shows, and dug through all the cupboards. I made a new collar for Molly out of braided shoelaces.

Boredom forced me to study the scribbles on the walls. They were scrawled everywhere—even on the handrails going upstairs. But as I studied them, I noticed a surprising neatness. The diagrams were carefully drawn. The circles were perfectly round. The equations were tidily stacked. The scribbles didn't look as crazy as I'd originally thought. Maybe they made sense after all.

I decided to find out if I was right. I scoured the house for a diagram simple enough for me to understand. I found an equation that read like this:

$$\mathcal{E}_k = \tfrac{1}{2} \times I \times w^2$$

I had no idea what that meant but next to the equation was this:

$$w = angular\ velocity$$

I = the moment of inertia of the mass at the center of rotation

That made no sense to me either. Below that, though, was an unexpectedly simple diagram. It featured a wooden spool, three heavy washers, a very sharp pencil, and a couple of rubber bands. I tried to create the device with stuff I found in our kitchen junk drawer. After three tries and forty-five minutes, I ended up with something that looked like a spinning top, so I twisted some string around the wooden spool and gave it a tug.

The top spun on the kitchen floor, tilt and all, for about ten minutes before it clattered onto its side and fell apart.

That simple little top made me smile. Something in this house, insignificant as it was, had actually worked the way I'd hoped it would. I looked around the house for another diagram I could decipher, but all of them baffled me.

"I'm bored again," I said.

"Why don't you go read something?" Mom was sorting through a box of photographs in the living room.

"I'm not in the mood."

"Enough already, Josh. Go play a game."

"Played them all."

"Then make yourself lunch. I've got some sliced provolone in the fridge. You could get a straw and poke little holes in it."

"I'm not hungry. And Aaron's the one who pokes holes in cheese. Not me."

"You're driving me crazy, Josh. There's got to be something in this house you can do."

I thought for a moment. "Can I go up to the attic?"

"Absolutely not. You'll get bitten by a rat."

"All the rats moved next door," I said. "Besides, I don't think Mr. Daga would ever bite me."

"Well, you'll get bitten by something."

"No, I won't. And Dad said there's still all sorts of weird old junk up there. Why can't I look through it?"

"Because I said so. You'd probably fall through the ceiling. Go do something else."

I shuffled up to my room and sat on the floor. I stared at the scribbles I hadn't managed to cover over with posters. I was studying a diagram of a holly berry next to the words *ilex aquifolium* when I heard the back door slam. That meant Mom had gone outside to work in the garden. An impulse I couldn't resist grabbed hold of me. I ran up the stairs to the All-the-Way-Up Room.

I opened the hidden door, clicked the switch, and watched a lone bulb blush to life somewhere back in the gloom.

The ceiling slanted low, forcing me to crouch. Stacks of boxes tilted everywhere, and shadowy shapes filled the corners. The attic space faded to blackness, far beyond the dim glow of the lightbulb.

I rushed back to my room and dug through my drawers until I found a headlamp I used for camping. I stood motionless and listened for a minute, but the house was quiet. Mom was still outside.

Using the headlamp to light the way, I crawled through the little door into the attic. In the boxes just inside the door I found:

- An old cloth flour bag full of pennies dated 1929. They all looked brand new, and there must have been a thousand of them.

- An envelope with old first, second, and third place ribbons for shot-putting at a New York high school track invitational.

- Boxes and boxes of books. Only two looked interesting—an old red book with an ornate cover decorated with gold holly leaves, and one called *Handbook of United States Coins*. Both were well chewed by rats.

- Coin albums completely devoid of coins. The rats had chewed these as well.

- A rusty three-inch pocketknife. I put this in my pocket.

- Seven wigs. They all fit me.

- A carpenter's level with a wedge of wood glued to the bottom on one end.

- A ship in a bottle. Only a jumble of wooden sticks and tangled string remained. Tiny rat droppings lay in the bottle, and I figured some of Mr. Daga's kids had played on the ship and wrecked it.

- Matches from a restaurant called the Alt Heidelberg.

All of these boxes sat within ten feet of the three-foot-high door. The attic went much farther back from that. I set the pennies and the wigs outside the door to play with later, took a deep breath, and began crawling into the darkness.

The attic was tucked into the eaves, framing the walls of the All-the-Way-Up Room. I crawled for twenty feet and then reached a corner. I leaned as far forward as I could and peeked slowly around. Cobwebs glowed white in the beam of my headlamp. I crawled to where the roof met the slanted attic floor and found an abandoned bird's nest surrounded by feathers and droppings. The floor creaked somewhere ahead. I glanced up and the light caught something white on a beam about twenty feet away. It looked like words.

The attic smelled like rat droppings, but I took a deep breath and crawled toward the words. Every few feet, I had to crawl through an old web. I imagined spiders scurrying down my back, and it made me shiver. Finally, I crawled close enough to make out the words "three o'clock."

I'd always liked three o'clock. That was when school let out. I took it as a good sign and crawled closer. The letters looked like they were written in white chalk. I searched the beams nearby, but there were no other words. I looked along the bottom of the crawl space, where the beam touched the floor. Still nothing. I looked at the wall directly to the right of the words. There, in the same spidery letters and the same white chalk, was written "nine o'clock."

All nine o'clock meant to me was bedtime on a school night. I wondered what the time meant to the person who'd written it here. I searched the area around wall and found nothing but more cobwebs.

I continued to crawl further into the darkness until I reached another corner. At that corner the floorboards stopped. The floor beams were spaced two feet apart with nothing between them but the plaster ceiling of the rooms below. I would have to crawl from beam to beam. If I missed a beam, I would fall through the ceiling. And if that happened Mom and Dad would kill me.

Every time a board creaked, my stomach flipped. Hundreds of cobwebs waited for me. I had just decided to turn back when I saw more letters. Halfway up the wall to my left was written "six o'clock." Directly below that, on one of the floor joists, was scribbled "nine o'clock."

Suddenly, the system made sense. The words were directions. On the face of a clock, three was on the right, nine was on the left, and six was straight down. All I had to do was imagine where the hour hand on a clock would point. But who had written the directions? And what did they lead to?

I had to keep going. I crawled carefully from tilting floor beam to tilting floor beam, balancing on my hands and knees to keep from falling through the plaster ceiling into the room below. Halfway along, I reached the word "midnight." Did midnight mean I should look straight ahead or straight up? I aimed my headlamp up but saw nothing. I shone it straight ahead and could barely make out another set of letters written on a beam far ahead.

I prayed I wouldn't slip as I stretched to reach each beam. My knees hurt. I finally made it to the words "six o'clock." I looked down.

Next to the beam was a little shelf. Resting on the shelf and hidden in the shadows sat a dust-covered metal box—it was about the size of Aaron's lunch box.

I tried to pick it up with one hand, but the box was surprisingly heavy. So, unsteadily balancing on my sore knees, I reached with both hands and grabbed the box.

I lost my balance.

With a crash, I hit the plaster and my legs broke through the ceiling of the room below. I was stuck waist deep in Tilton House.

THE BOX

THE ATTIC FILLED WITH DUST. Light shone up from the room below. The heavy box was still in my hands.

I listened for Mom's voice or the sound of her footsteps. Nothing. I looked down. Splintered wood and plaster jabbed my waist, keeping me from falling. It hurt. Very carefully, I set the box down on the nearest beam and tried to pull myself up and out. The plaster and wood cut deeper into me. I tried to twist around, but I was lodged tightly.

If I called Mom for help, she'd yell at me. And she'd call Dad for sure. But even if I could manage to get out on my own, there was no way I could hide that hole.

"Mom?" I called softly into the cobwebs and dust of the attic. No response. "Mom!" I shouted. Still nothing. I yelled at the top of my lungs. I yelled for minutes on end. "Mom! Help!" No one came.

Maybe no one would ever come. Maybe I'd be stuck here until the batteries ran out on my headlamp. Maybe spiders were crawling over my head right now, getting ready to sink their fangs into me. I ran my hands through my hair in a panic.

The house held me tight. And not in a comforting way. "You may not always like me," the house seemed to be saying, "but you're not going anywhere and neither am I."

Finally, after what felt like half an hour, I heard a noise below that sounded like the back door slamming.

"Josh?" came the distant sound of Mom's voice.

"I'm up here!" I yelled.

The voice came closer. "I was in the backyard. Did you call me?"

"Yes!"

"Is everything all right?"

"No."

I heard the sound of hurrying footsteps on the stairs, then Mom's voice directly below me. "Oh my Lord. Are you hurt?"

"I'm stuck."

Mom called Dad, who came home in spite of the measles quarantine. After an hour of careful cutting with a saw, I fell into Dad's arms. Red scrapes circled my waist. I tried to play them off as no big deal, but they really hurt. Mom yelled at me for disobeying her order to stay out of the attic, and Dad yelled at me for making the hole in the ceiling and forcing him to come home from work in the middle of the day. Then Mom hugged me for a while and sprayed a bunch of Bactine on my scrapes, which isn't supposed to hurt but always stings like crazy anyway. Dad said we would talk later about consequences, but he had to return to work before he got in trouble with Mr. Stevens.

I had grabbed the box before Dad pulled me out. Dad barely looked at it, probably because he was in such a hurry to get back to work.

Dad, Grandpa, and Aaron returned home the next day. When they pulled up in front of Tilton House, I went outside for the first time since the measles began.

After Dad helped him out of the car, Grandpa stared at the house and whistled. "You done good, son." I turned. Dad had nearly finished painting during my quarantine. Now the house had bright white trim and shutters against rich gray-blue walls. It looked all dressed up and ready to meet the mayor.

Dad smiled proudly. I smiled, too. The house still looked crazy on the inside, but I was kind of proud of how it looked on the outside.

Dad and Grandpa set about patching the hole in the ceiling with boards, sheetrock, and plaster. I had to help and also had to pay for part of the supplies out of my allowance. I didn't mind. I figured I owed the house that much.

"Promise me you won't go into the attic anymore," Mom said.

"I don't want you making any more holes," said Dad. "I got enough work around here as it is."

"Which reminds me," said Mom. "When are you going to paint the inside of this place?"

"I haven't photographed the walls yet," replied Dad as he walked away, "but don't worry. It's on my to-do list."

Aaron and I examined the metal box on my first break from helping patch the ceiling. The box was olive green and heavy and, unlike most boxes, didn't open at the top. Instead, there were two drawers under a keyhole. The metalwork around the keyhole was shaped like a capital T.

I pulled the bottom drawer, but it wouldn't open. Then I pulled the top one and it slid out smoothly. Inside lay a paper envelope and a tiny key. The handle of the key was shaped like the T around the keyhole, but the key was far too small to fit in the lock.

I tried anyway. It didn't work.

"Maybe you have to turn the key sideways," said Aaron.

I tried that. Then I tried putting the key in backward. Nothing worked. I picked up the envelope from the drawer and read the spidery writing on it out loud:

Warning! Grow Powder! Deadly consequences! Contains quadratically ionized ilex aquifolium. Extremely dangerous! Use far away from all animals and humans.

"What's 'grow powder'?" asked Aaron.

As soon as Aaron said that, I understood. "It's to make the key grow!" I said. "You put grow powder on the key and it will grow until it fits the lock."

"How do you know?"

"Why else would the key and the envelope be together?"

"That is so cool," said Aaron. "We could sprinkle some on a Hot Wheels car. Then we could have our own cars." We both stared at the envelope in silence for a moment and thought about the possibilities of the grow powder. "Why does it say it has 'deadly consequences'?"

"Well, what if it makes the key grow to five times its normal size?" I said. "Or ten times? Or what if you accidentally spilled some on a dog and it grew to the size of a horse?"

Aaron's face went white. He hated dogs.

"That's why we can't open it now," I said, slipping the tiny envelope back into the metal drawer. "We need to wait until we're way out in the middle of nowhere, where nothing bad like that could happen. Someplace safe."

MOSS

WE NEEDED TO GET FAR AWAY from civilization. Far away from dogs and cats and rats and other things that could grow big and dangerous. I talked to Dad at breakfast the next day.

"Don't you think your poor, recovering son should get out of the house?"

Dad grunted and kept eating his cereal and reading the paper.

"I'll take that as a yes," I said. "Think about all that time Mom spent alone with me. She probably needs a break, because I think I was driving her crazy."

"What do you want, Josh?" Dad said, without raising his eyes from his paper.

"I was thinking it would be fun to go on a boys' hiking trip this weekend."

Dad looked up at me and said, "You're right. That would be fun."

After dinner that night, he packed our pickup with gear.

It didn't turn out fun at all.

We were pulling the packs from our truck at the trailhead when a forest ranger walked up. His beard looked like the moss that hangs from old trees.

"How you doin', folks?" he said cheerily.

"Fine," muttered Dad. He hated seeing other people when we went hiking. "The whole reason you go hiking is to get away from other humans," Dad always said. The sight of a single soda can or cigarette butt could ruin his whole weekend. If Dad spotted another hiker, he would walk straight ahead without a word, trying to pretend the person wasn't there.

The ranger took Dad's rudeness in stride. "Well, be sure you stay on the trail," he said. "This is an awfully remote area. There's no one to help if you get in trouble. Hardly ever come out here myself."

"Good," said Dad. He pulled the pack onto his back and walked up the trail. Aaron and I had to scramble to catch up.

It had taken us about six hours to drive to the trailhead from Tilton House in Tacoma. Now we were hiking toward a campsite in the Olympic National Forest, near the Dosewallips River and one of Grandpa's favorite fishing spots.

One-hundred-foot-high cedar and fir trees cast the Olympic National Forest in shadow. Soggy, seaweed-colored moss hangs from the branches and droopy ferns cover the ground. At least, that's how I remember it. I've never been back since that trip. I'll never go back.

An hour later, we still hadn't seen another sign of human life and Dad's mood had improved. The trail was poorly marked and barely maintained, so every half hour we'd stop and Dad would check our progress on his trail map. Each time we took a break, I would take my pack off for a few minutes. I had the metal box hidden under my sleeping bag and it was heavy.

We walked for two hours until lunchtime. While Dad was fixing cheese sandwiches, I sat next to Aaron to firm up our plans.

"Tonight, as soon as Dad goes to sleep, we use the grow powder on the key," I whispered.

"Does it have to be in the dark?" Aaron asked.

"Don't be a baby."

After lunch, we put in another four hours of steady hiking before Dad said we should set up camp. "With trees this tall and thick, it'll get dark early."

He pulled out his map again and studied the contour lines, looking for a likely spot. "That's funny," he said. "This next part of the map is blank."

"What do you mean?" I asked.

"Look," Dad said, pointing at the map. "We're here. This red line marks the trail and all these curvy brown lines show the contour of the land. The closer they are together, the steeper the land is. But up around this little bend, the lines disappear."

"Maybe it's real flat there," said Aaron. "That might be a good place to pitch our tent."

"Maybe. Or it could be that they didn't print that part of the map because no one has ever mapped it."

"Well, the trail doesn't go through it," I said, "so if we stay on the trail, we should be fine."

69

Dad looked at us gravely and put a hand on both of our shoulders. "Josh, Aaron, I think you're missing something. What we have here is an opportunity. We've stumbled upon uncharted territory. Not much of that left these days. Nearly every square inch of this earth has been tromped over, littered upon, photographed, documented, and generally soaked in the stench of human activity. Now, it could just be that this map is a bad printout, but it's also possible that we have found a few acres of land no one has ever mapped before. Maybe no one has ever even set foot on it. Think of it. This may be the only chance in our lives to step into the unknown."

"The ranger said we should stay on the trail," said Aaron.

"Sure he did. And that's good advice, too. Stay on the trail. Play it safe. Turn your back on your chance for discovery. That's what we should probably do. Right, boys?"

"Right!" said Aaron enthusiastically. I nodded.

"Noooo! No, no, no! You're not getting it!" Dad shouted, waving his arms around and pacing up and down the trail. "Forget the trail. Forget the dadblamed map! We're striking out on our own. 'O brave new world' and all that! Tonight, we camp in a new land! Come on!"

What could we do? We followed Dad around a bend in the trail until, according to the map, the uncharted territory was directly to our left. If that part of the land had never been mapped, I could see why. Bushes and nettles and brambles covered it so densely, it looked like it would take a bulldozer to cut through it. But Dad didn't hesitate. He stepped over the stinging nettles and plowed into the bushes.

After fifteen minutes, we were still barely fifty feet from the trail. Thorns caught our clothes and scratched our skin. Thick

70

branches blocked our path, and the farther we went, the soggier the ground got. Finally, the underbrush thinned and the bushes gave way to huge ferns and leggy rhododendrons. The ground was still soggy, but it rose just ahead. If we climbed up that hill, Dad said, we would probably reach drier ground.

We made it to the top of the hill and stopped. Dad whistled. "Wow," Aaron said. I agreed. Wow. We were looking at one of the most beautiful places I'd ever seen.

Aaron named it the Mossy Spot and we claimed it on behalf of Tilton House.

The Mossy Spot consisted of a clearing about four times as wide as our tent, ringed by ancient-looking Douglas fir trees. Everything in the clearing was smothered in thick emerald moss. Everything. There were no bare patches and no other plants— only moss. The moss grew about twenty feet up the trees. It grew over every bump on the ground, large or small. It was so green that I kind of wanted to take a bite to see what it tasted like.

"*This* is where we are camping tonight," said Dad.

At that moment, I was glad we'd left the trail. As I stared at this untouched morsel of the world, all the scratches on my arms from plowing through the brush didn't matter.

When we stepped into the clearing, the spongy moss felt like pillows under our feet. Dad and Aaron dropped their packs and Dad began to unroll our tent. I hesitated before taking off my own pack. The Mossy Spot seemed like the kind of place you should look at and maybe photograph, then leave without making a single mark. But Dad seemed determined to camp there.

He handed me the hatchet and I began pounding the tent stakes through the previously unscarred moss. When the first stake went in, I flinched a little. Or maybe it was the ground that flinched. It felt like I was poking a pin into flesh.

By the time we had the tent raised and our sleeping bags rolled out, it was growing dark. Dad fired up the camp stove and boiled some water. I noticed that we were all trying not to make a sound. Our voices felt too much like an intrusion. So we sat inside the tent and ate warm noodles in silence. As soon as the sun went down, the Mossy Spot turned chilly, so we climbed inside our sleeping bags. The moss felt like a thick feather bed beneath us. For some reason it made me wonder if flies felt this comfortable when they first landed on a spiderweb.

"Hey, Dad. Tell us a scary story," said Aaron. "Tell us 'The Golden Arm.'"

"Not gonna happen," said Dad. "Last time I told that story, you had nightmares for a week and I got in serious Dutch with your mother."

"Besides, this place is scary enough as it is," I said.

Aaron sighed, then pulled out a book from his pack and began to read. Dad and I did the same, reading in the lantern light on the soft moss, in the warmth of our sleeping bags. Aaron and I exchanged glances. We knew it wouldn't take long for Dad to nod off, and then we'd have our chance to try out the grow powder on the key. Soon he closed his book and turned on his side. In less then ten minutes, Dad was snoring softly.

Aaron whispered, "Get the box."

I dug it out of my pack with a grunt.

"Let's go outside so we don't spill any on the tent," I said.

"Or on Dad," said Aaron ominously.

Dad snored on, unaware that a little carelessness from us might turn him into a giant.

Aaron picked up the lantern. We quietly unzipped the tent flap and climbed outside. The lantern light only carried a few feet into the darkness. I held the metal box as Aaron set the lantern on the ground and cautiously opened the top drawer. He took out the envelope and key and held them carefully in his hands. "You want to do it?"

"Only if you want me to."

"I want you to." His hands were shaking. I tried to steady my own hands as I handed Aaron the box and took the envelope and the key. I reached into my pocket and pulled out the tiny pocketknife.

"Is that Dad's?" Aaron asked.

"No. I found it in the attic." I opened the blade and used it to peel back the flap. A teaspoon of tan powder lay inside the envelope.

"It looks like sawdust," I said.

"What now?" Aaron asked.

I thought for a moment, then slid the tiny knife blade through the key's handle. I dipped the key and knife into the envelope, saying, "This way, we won't spill any."

But as soon as they touched the powder, both the key and the knife grew five times their size. I was so startled that I dropped the key and the envelope. "Get back!" I yelled. "Whatever you do, don't get any of that powder on you!"

The key lay on the moss. It looked like it had grown to the perfect size for the metal box. I reached to pick it up, but before I could, moss covered it.

The moss was growing.

I stepped back toward the tent in surprise. With the metal box still clutched in his hands, Aaron ran in the opposite direction, out of the glow of the lantern. A moment later I heard him yelp.

"What's going on out there?" mumbled Dad behind me.

"Help!" Aaron cried. Dad had pulled aside the tent flaps and was kneeling beside me. "Aaron?" he called, looking out. "Josh, where's your brother? What's going on?"

Before I could answer, the lantern grew dim. In seconds, the light changed to an emerald glow and then went out. Moss had completely engulfed it.

"Get in the tent, Josh," Dad said. I did. He quickly pulled on his boots and climbed outside. I heard him call, "Aaron! Aaron! Aaron! Aaaaarrronnnn!" His voice became muffled. Then silence.

My little brother and dad had disappeared in the darkness outside. What was I supposed to do? I realized I was still holding on to what had once been a tiny pocketknife. It was now the size of a machete. I dug through my pack and found my flashlight. I shone it at the door of the tent. Moss was moving quickly across the floor. I slashed at it with the knife, struggling not to scream. I tried to step outside, but the moss immediately began growing over my shoes and up my legs. I slashed at the moss on my shoes and the floor of the tent. I tore my feet free and climbed outside.

"Dad?" I called. "Aaron?" No answer. I aimed the flashlight around the clearing. My hand was shaking so hard that the beam was jumping all over. I saw two shapes, one tall and one short. Both were completely covered in moss.

I tried to take a step toward them, but my feet wouldn't move. I shone the beam down and saw that the moss was growing up my legs again and had reached my knees. I screamed and hacked away at it with the knife. I knew I was cutting my legs, but I was so intent on freeing myself from the moss that I felt nothing.

I kept slashing and peeling the moss off my legs, but it grew as fast as I could cut it away. I slashed my way over to Dad and

Aaron. I began cutting and scraping at the tall shape, jumping up and down to keep the moss from catching hold of my feet. At last, I peeled away a fist-sized section and Dad's face broke through with a gasp. He stared at me wild-eyed a moment before he finally appeared to recognize me.

"Cut me loose!" he cried.

I cut and peeled until his arms broke free. He took the knife from me and began hacking at his feet like a wild man, cursing the moss and praying to God in the same ragged breaths. We both jumped and thrashed around like we were on fire, trying to keep the moss from catching hold. We made our way to Aaron and Dad scraped at Aaron's face until he'd bared my brother's mouth and nose. Aaron's head fell limply to his chest.

"Stand close to me!" Dad called as I kept jumping from one foot to the other. He continued working at Aaron's feet. Aaron started to cough. His eyes opened. Blood was running down his cheek where Dad had cut him while scraping away moss.

Dad spun me around and faced me the way we had come. "Shine your flashlight that way, Josh." I did. I could see a pyramid-shaped hill of moss where our tent had been.

"Now we run for it," said Dad as he gave one final slash to free Aaron's feet. "I'll go first with the knife and clear a path. Josh, you keep Aaron in between us and shine your light in front of me as best you can. No one stops running until we hit the trail."

The moss grabbed at our feet, but between our fear-fueled speed and Dad's sweeping slashes, we managed to cross the clearing and plow back down the hillside and through the bushes. We reached the trail, scratched and bleeding.

Our packs and tent were buried back at the Mossy Spot. There was nothing to do but hike to the trailhead in the cold and dark.

Just as dawn was breaking, we reached our pickup truck, where Dad bandaged my legs and Aaron's cheek as best he could.

It wasn't until we were in the pickup driving home that Dad mentioned the metal box Aaron still had in his hands, and the huge knife.

"You want to tell me about these?" he said quietly. We didn't. It would have meant telling him that our curiosity had nearly killed us. But in the end, we told him everything.

"Unmarked territory," Dad muttered. "And I thought I was the one taking chances."

THE DIMMER SWITCH

As soon as we returned from the camping trip, Mom hustled us back into the car and drove us straight to Dr. Trumble's office. He stitched up two cuts on my leg and a deep one on Aaron's cheek. We both were going to have scars. Aaron was thrilled—he thought it would make him look like a pirate.

The metal box sat unopened on our bedroom dresser. The box was built as solid as a safe, and its key was lost forever under the moss. I asked Lola to come over to take a shot at it.

Lola had never been in our house before. I watched her nervously as she walked through the front door. She stumbled a bit on the tilting floor and then stood as still as a marble statue as her eyes scanned the words, numbers, and diagrams on the walls. A smile flitted across her face, but she hid it quickly.

"It's even weirder than I thought," she said.

We went up to my room and tried prying the box open, but we succeeded only in breaking one of Dad's best screwdrivers and one of Mom's butter knives. Lola ran home and came back with one of her mom's oyster forks. We broke that, too. Her mom noticed. Apparently, she polishes the silverware once a week.

We took a break from the box and went outside to ride bikes until dinnertime. When Mom called us in, I left my bike lying on our front lawn, just a few feet from our porch steps. When I went out to get it after dinner, it was gone. I was sure I knew who'd stolen it.

The Purple Door Man collected junk and hated kids. He wasn't one of those guys who seemed grumpy until you got to know him and then realized he was gruff but lovable. He was gruff all right, but he definitely wasn't lovable. At least once a day, he yelled at us to stop making so much noise.

But that's not all he did. He stole from us.

To be fair to the Purple Door Man, it started with the toys we left in front of his house. We'd step inside for lunch and come back out to find our Frisbee or football gone.

At first, we figured some kid cruising through our neighborhood had picked them up. Or maybe we had left them somewhere else. Then it started happening more often and it started happening even if the toys had been in our yard.

Now, two weeks after the horrible camping trip, my bike disappeared from in front of our house.

I felt sick. It was the middle of summer. My birthday and Christmas were months away, and here I was stuck with nothing to ride.

The Purple Door Man yelled to me from his front porch, "Sad about your bike, eh, sonny?"

"What? Did you see who took it?" I asked anxiously.

"I'm not sayin'," he said, "but it serves you right for all the noise you kids are always makin'!"

From the way the Purple Door Man said this, I knew he'd been the one who'd stolen my bike. He smiled.

In less than a week, Aaron's and Lola's bikes disappeared, too.

I told Mom about my suspicion. She frowned and said it might be so. She even said she would talk to the Purple Door Man, but I could tell she didn't think it would do much good.

Then something happened that night that made Mom forget all about our bikes. That was the night we ordered pizza from Big Sam's Pizzeria.

The pizza we ordered never arrived. After ninety minutes, I called the restaurant to complain. Big Sam apologized and told me, "Don't worry, little one. Big Sam's policy is 'If the pizza isn't delivered in half an hour, you don't have to pay.'" He asked for precise directions, which we gave him, but still the delivery guy never showed. We couldn't have known it had something to do with the way Dad wired the dimmer switch in the dining room.

A dimmer switch is a kind of light switch with a dial that you can turn down to dim the light or up to brighten it. At least, that's how they usually work.

When Dad had started installing the switch in our dining room that Saturday afternoon, Mom had told him he should ask Mr. Daga for help. "Be honest, dear. Do you have any idea what you're doing? We live right next door to someone who not only knows about electricity but has proved he knows about the wiring of *this house,* and he's offered to help you anytime you need it. I don't understand why you won't him ask for help!"

Dad muttered a few things I couldn't hear and insisted on wiring the switch on his own. But the lights in the chandelier above the dining table refused to turn on. The switch wouldn't work. At least not the way dimmer switches usually work.

Dad put his tools away and turned the switch all the way off. Since the pizza never arrived, we ate cheese sandwiches for dinner instead.

The next morning, Dad, Aaron, Grandpa, and I woke up to Mom screaming. We ran downstairs and found her leaning against the closed front door, her face white as a glass of skim milk.

"Something's . . . wrong . . . outside" was all she could manage.

"What do you mean?" said Dad.

"I went out to the porch to get the paper. But . . . it's missing," she said.

"The paper is missing?" asked Dad.

"No. The porch. Look." She opened the door.

Mom was right. The porch was gone. Instead, the doorway opened to a four foot drop to the ground. The morning paper, meanwhile, floated level with our front door.

Dad tried to step down to investigate, but his foot stopped in midair, at the height of the front door. He tapped his foot against something, then stepped out onto an invisible platform. It looked like he was suspended in space.

"I don't think the porch is gone," said Dad, awe in his voice. "I think it's invisible."

Grandpa leaned his wooden leg out the doorway. His wooden foot went *tap, tap, tap,* against nothing we could see.

Dad inched his way across the invisible porch, down invisible

80

steps, all the way down to the visible front yard. When he turned to face the house, he gasped. "Oh, my. Come and look."

Aaron and I carefully made our way to the yard. We turned and faced the house. It was gone. Mom and Grandpa floated in the open front door, with the hallway and kitchen still visible behind them. Dad tried to reassure Mom by jumping up and down on the invisible porch. He even felt his way over to the invisible porch swing, sat down in it, and started swinging. It looked pretty weird.

"Maybe we can paint it," Dad said.

"You just finished painting it, Hal!" said Mom with a sob. Then she slammed the door shut. From where we stood, our house now looked like it didn't exist.

We were standing in the front yard discussing what to do when Mrs. Natalie came over from next door. "What the heck happened to your house, Hal?" she asked. Dad said he didn't know what had happened and that the house was still there even though no one could see it. Mrs. Natalie raised her eyebrows. Dad stepped up to the invisible porch and walked across it. Mrs. Natalie raised her eyebrows even more. Dad felt around, then opened the front door, which looked to be attached to nothing, and Mrs. Natalie could see our hallway, same as ever, except that it was floating four feet in the air. She raised her eyebrows even higher until her eyes rolled back inside her head. With a ladylike groan, she passed out right on the grass.

All the neighbors kept coming over, asking what had happened to our house. Dad kept trying to explain, walking around on the porch to show them it was still there. I could tell he was getting tired of it. At one point, while all the grown-ups were standing around talking, two boys from another neighborhood rode by on their bikes and tried to cut through what must have looked like our vacant lot. Too late, I yelled, "Watch out!" They crashed into the side of our invisible house. Dad marched over to the boys, who were sitting on the ground looking stunned and said, "There's a house there, you know."

Dad's mood grew even worse after his boss, Mr. Stevens, finally came by to take a look at all the scribbles on our walls. Mr. Stevens's face was so tan and round, it looked like a basketball with eyes. When he saw—or didn't see—our house, he frowned and said, "This isn't the kind of publicity we need right now, Hal." As if Dad had intentionally turned our house invisible. Dad promised to take care of it, then started grumbling as soon as Mr. Stevens left. He hadn't even come inside to see the diagrams and writings.

Aaron, Lola, and I spent most of that Sunday opening and closing the invisible front door, climbing in and out of the invisible windows, and leaning against the invisible walls. It looked so cool. Overnight, Tilton House had turned into something out of a science fiction movie.

Grandpa sat on the invisible porch swing all day, throwing out different questions and theories to Dad: "Have you checked with the city?" "Maybe you forgot to pay your cable bill." "It's probably some kind of government experiment we don't know about."

I liked throwing a football through the front door, because if you stood outside at just the right angle, the football seemed to disappear. Aaron kept asking me to open and close the upstairs windows. He said it looked like a square of our house popped right out of the sky. Mom and Dad wanted the old house back, but I hoped Tilton House would stay invisible forever. "Think how awesome it would look if it snowed," I said to Lola.

"My mom says it's going to lower the neighborhood property values," she said. "And it could be dangerous. Do you have any idea what made your house disappear? What if it's contagious? What if tomorrow *you* wake up invisible?"

"You're just jealous," I said. Lola stared at me in silence, then turned on her heel and walked to her neat, level, visible home.

I went inside to look at something I'd remembered seeing scrawled on one of our walls. It was right above the top of the couch.

Invisibility, electricity, and the refractive index of air.

The writing beneath that mentioned something called Snell's Law, which made it clear that given the precisely correct conditions, light could be bent backward upon itself, rendering objects undetectable to the human eye. Next to the text was a complicated wiring diagram. I studied the diagram, wondering if it would explain how the house became invisible.

Mom stayed inside the entire day, talking on the phone to her friends about what had happened. She never once walked across the invisible porch. She answered a call from a newspaper reporter who wanted to stop by to take pictures, and she seemed excited about that—I know Aaron and I were. Since there was no house, she said she didn't know what the reporter planned to take pictures of. She said it would make more sense if a TV crew came so they could film Dad walking across the porch or swinging in the swing. Dad seemed less excited. I guess he was remembering what Mr. Stevens had said about bad publicity for the museum. He called the reporter back and asked him not to come. The reporter said he appreciated the call and hung up.

Since Dad couldn't fix the house's invisibility, he tried to fix the dimmer switch instead. He fiddled with it that night after dinner, but the chandelier still wouldn't work, so he quit, unknowingly leaving the dimmer switch turned halfway up. We couldn't tell from the inside, but from the outside, our house was now halfway visible. You could see it, but at the same time you could see through it to the backyard. That's how it looked the next morning when the newspaper reporter arrived with a camera slung around his neck. Dad met him outside and asked him not to take pictures, as it would cause Dad trouble at work. The reporter, whose name was Van Leopold, nodded his head but started taking pictures anyway.

That picture covered the front page of the local paper the next day. Most people thought the photograph was a fake, but Dad said that wouldn't help matters with Mr. Stevens. On top of that, the article mentioned that Dad was the curator of the art museum.

After the reporter left, we were all having lunch in the kitchen when Aaron mentioned that the house looked "like it was dimmed." Mom frowned at Aaron, dashed into the dining room, and turned the dimmer switch all the way up. She ran to the front door, threw it open, and looked outside. "Hah!" she yelled triumphantly, jumping up and down. "I knew it! The house is back! My beautiful house!"

Sure enough, the house was visible again.

Dad couldn't believe the dimmer switch had caused all this trouble, so he went back to the dining room to test it by turning the switch off again, but Mom yelled at him from the porch, "Don't you dare touch that switch, Hal! Nobody touches that switch! And next time you put one in, you're getting Mr. Daga to help you!"

Mom covered the switch with duct tape to keep anyone from turning it. We've never touched it since. Well, almost never.

Sometimes when we order a pizza from Big Sam's, I might untape the switch and turn it down, but only for half an hour. Because as Big Sam says, "If the pizza isn't delivered in half an hour, you don't have to pay."

MRS. NATALIE'S LITTLE WHITE DOG

FOR AARON, IT WAS LOVE at first sight.

The object of his affection was Mrs. Natalie's new dog. Mrs. Natalie had grown lonely since Mr. Natalie's death, so it didn't surprise us when she came over one day to introduce Dinky, a Maltese, as white as a puffy cloud and only a little bigger than a house cat. Before Dinky came along, Aaron had hated dogs. But Dinky immediately won him over by being so small and cute.

For Dinky, it was love at first sniff. I don't think she'd ever smelled an eight-year-old boy before. Aaron always had something sticky in his pocket or on his hands. And Aaron wanted to play. Her owner may have been a nice old lady, but Dinky's heart belonged to Aaron. Luckily, Dinky's jumping and barking and chewing wore Mrs. Natalie out, so she always seemed happy for a break when Aaron came by.

Dinky chewed on everything, barked at everything, ran circles around everything, and did it all at full speed. Mrs. Natalie put up with her because Dinky always seemed happy, and Mrs. Natalie needed happiness around her.

But it was my brother who made Dinky happiest of all. If he took a single step outside Tilton House, Dinky would explode out of the little doggie door that Mrs. Natalie had asked Grandpa to install. She would run at Aaron, jump all over him, bark with joy, and wiggle uncontrollably for five minutes. Aaron would dash around the block with Dinky giving chase, or the pair would wrestle on the grass or sprawl on the living room floor as Dinky and her sharp teeth destroyed another pair of shoes.

When I appeared, she would run at me and jump on me for ten seconds or so. Same with Lola or Mom or Dad. But she'd always return to Aaron. If she could, she'd be touching him at all times, pressed against his leg or wiggling all over his lap.

Late one afternoon, Lola and I were sitting on the floor in my bedroom, trying to open the bottom drawer of the metal box that I had found in the attic. Aaron was on his side of the room speaking to Dinky as if she were a human.

"*Ilex aquifolium,*" said Aaron, slowly reading the words written on the bedroom ceiling. "Can you say that, Dinky?" Dinky responded with pants and growls.

"Who do you think put the grow powder in this box?" asked Lola.

"I figure it has to be the same guy who wrote all over the walls."

"But why would he go to all the trouble of hiding the box in the attic? And of using a tiny key to lock it?" Lola looked up from fiddling with the box. "Do you have a knife or something?"

"Do I ever have a knife!" I reached under my bed to pull out the machete-sized pocketknife. It wasn't there. I bent down to look and saw something about the size of Grandpa's lighter. I pulled it out. It was the knife, but it was tiny again.

"It shrank!" I said.

"No, it's perfect," said Lola. She tried to insert the tip of the knife into the seams of the box, but the box was so well built that even the tiny knife couldn't penetrate.

When Lola turned the box upside down to examine the under-side, scraps from the envelope that had contained the growth powder fell to the floor. In a flash, Dinky zipped across the room and started eating the bits of paper.

"Smart dog you have there," said Lola.

"He is smart," said Aaron. "And since you think you're so smart, he's not even a he. He's a she."

Lola grunted and turned her attention back to the metal box. I rolled onto my back and stared at the ceiling, wondering how I could prove that the Purple Door Man had stolen our bikes. I could still hear Aaron and Dinky happily growling and talking to each other. Dinky's growls rose in pitch, as if her tail had been stepped on. Then they took on a gargly tone before stopping altogether. I rolled over to see what was going on, and sat up immediately. Dinky's eyes were bulging and her tongue hung out of her mouth.

"Your genius dog is choking," said Lola.

"Mind your own beeswax," said Aaron, but he looked scared.

"I'm not kidding." Lola dropped the metal box and grabbed Dinky. "Aaron! He's choking! Why'd you make his collar so tight?"

I picked up the knife from the floor and started sawing at the collar.

"I didn't touch her collar!" Aaron shrieked.

All at once, the collar broke with a snap. Dinky started coughing and shaking. She panted a few times, then wriggled free from Lola and ran into Aaron's arms as if nothing had happened.

"A real smart dog you have there," said Lola. "Not only does he eat paper, but he chokes himself, too."

"He's a *she!*" said Aaron.

From downstairs, Mom yelled that it was time for dinner. Aaron walked Dinky back to Mrs. Natalie for the night.

The next morning, Aaron and I hung around in the living room, playing Monopoly. At about eleven, I was winning when Mom chased us outside into the sunshine. As soon as we were in the front yard, we heard Dinky barking. Her head popped out of her doggie door, then her front feet. Then she stopped. She barked again. Her furry body completely filled the door. She wiggled, barked, and strained against the door until the rest of her body followed. She bounced down the porch steps and ran over to Aaron.

"She grew!" said Aaron. He was right. Yesterday, Dinky had been the size of a cat. Now she came up to Aaron's knees.

"That's weird," I said. "She didn't seem nearly this big yesterday."

"I bet it's because she ate that paper envelope yesterday. The one that had the grow powder in it," said Aaron.

"I hope she doesn't get any bigger," I said. What I really hoped was that the grown-ups wouldn't notice.

Aaron pulled a Frisbee out of a bush and tossed it. "Go get it, Dinky!" Dinky ran after the Frisbee, caught it as it bounced off the sidewalk, and instantly chewed it to pieces.

"Dang it, Aaron, that's mine!" I said. "Go get it back before she destroys it."

"Too late," Aaron said as Dinky tore a chunk out of the Frisbee.

"You owe me a new Frisbee," I said.

"I didn't do it!"

"Your dog did!"

"She's not my dog. She's Mrs. Natalie's."

I left Aaron with his furry friend and walked down to Lola's house. While I quietly told Lola about the growing dog, Lola's mom made us lunch—cucumber sandwiches on whole wheat bread, cut in perfect fourths and served with carrot sticks and apple slices. It wasn't too bad, but Lola's mom stood by the sink and watched us eat. She kept reminding Lola to eat over her plate so that she didn't get crumbs on the floor. As far as I could tell, Lola was eating over her plate the whole time. I finally figured out that I was the one dropping crumbs but Lola's mom was too polite to say anything to me.

We played with Lola's rock collection for a while. For rocks, they were pretty interesting. When we got back to my house, Aaron was still outside with Dinky.

"She's growing!" he yelled at us as we approached. "Look! Her back comes almost up to my waist!"

"Holy cow!" said Lola. "How big do you think she'll get?"

We brought Dinky back to Mrs. Natalie's, but the doggie door was far too small for her now. She'd grown up to *my* waist by then. Aaron opened Mrs. Natalie's front door to let the dog in and we heard Mrs. Natalie scream. Aaron said, "It's okay. She's still Dinky. She just grew."

I got a sick feeling in my stomach thinking back about the moss. What had we done to Dinky? I swallowed hard, grabbed Aaron, and we walked back home to tell Dad our theory. He listened to us silently. He didn't say a word during dinner, either. When we were done, Aaron and I went with him to talk to Mrs. Natalie.

"Thanks for coming over, Hal," said Mrs. Natalie, opening the door. "Get down, Dinky. I wanted to ask your opinion about—stop it now! I said get down!—about this—now you let go of his arm!—about this dog. She's grown so big so fast, I don't quite know what—Dinky, you are being a naughty puppy—I don't quite know what to—bad puppy!"

Dinky didn't seem to realize that she was now a big dog: She still jumped on everyone. She still chewed on everything. Except now she probably weighed seventy-five pounds. When she was tiny, she was only annoying. Now she was scary.

Dad sat Mrs. Natalie in a chair and began making her a cup of tea. He told Aaron to try to play with Dinky quietly until Mrs. Natalie had a chance to calm down. The next day was a Saturday and Dad promised he'd take Dinky to the vet. We returned home. Dad never mentioned a thing about the grow powder to Mrs. Natalie.

"It's all gone now, isn't it?" he said to Aaron and me as we stood on the porch.

"Is what all gone?"

"That powder, Josh."

"Yes. Even the envelope is gone."

Dad nodded and entered the house.

We were only partway through breakfast the next morning when the phone rang. I could hear Mrs. Natalie's frantic voice on the other end of the line. "Hal, I don't know what to do with this dog—" Then the phone went dead. We all ran next door—even Grandpa—but when we got to the front steps, we saw a huge wet nose and mouth poking through the doggie door. The mouth held the remains of Mrs. Natalie's phone. Mrs. Natalie's front door shook and strained against its hinges. We could hear Mrs. Natalie's hysterical voice from inside as she tried to get Dinky under control. Then the door burst open and the biggest, fluffiest dog I'd ever seen jumped off the porch and onto Aaron, knocking him to the ground. Dinky stood on top of him, her huge front paws on his chest, chewing happily on Mrs. Natalie's phone.

Aaron burst into tears. Who could blame him? Dinky was huge. The top of her head came up to my chin. She must have weighed three hundred pounds—maybe not as big as a pony, but bigger than any Saint Bernard I'd ever seen.

Dad and Mom pulled Dinky off of Aaron. At Dad's request, I ran to the garage for some rope. Dad and Grandpa did their best to hold on to the giant dog until I came back, and then Dad tied one end of the rope around her neck and the other end around the holly tree in Mrs. Natalie's front yard. Dinky strained against it, and for a minute I thought she would rip the tree out of the ground, but it held.

"What am I supposed to do with this thing?" asked Mrs. Natalie to no one in particular.

Dinky dropped the phone from her mouth and barked—a huge, deep sound that rattled my rib cage. Her dark, shiny eyes looked longingly at Aaron.

"She's not a thing," said Aaron, wiping the tears from his face. "She's still Dinky. She's just big."

"Mrs. Natalie didn't mean anything by it, Aaron," said Grandpa. "It's just that Dinky is a mighty large dog for one little lady."

"I suppose I should call the shelter," said Mrs. Natalie.

"No!" shouted Aaron. "You can't do that to Dinky!"

"I'm sorry, Aaron," said Mrs. Natalie, "but honestly, I don't know what else to do. I can't keep a dog this big. Especially when she's so naughty. Come and see what she did to my house."

We followed Mrs. Natalie inside. She led us into her kitchen, where she pointed to the spot where her phone used to hang from the wall. Now there was a ragged hole and dangling wires. All the knobs had been chewed off the kitchen cabinets, even the ones above the counters. In the living room, the back of the sofa was torn open and the heavy wooden frame was scarred with teeth marks.

Grandpa took Mrs. Natalie by the arm and led her over to our house. We all sat around the kitchen table, discussing what could be done with Dinky and trying to comfort Mrs. Natalie. Aaron stayed outside with Dinky. Someone had to comfort her too, he said.

The adult conversation grew boring pretty fast, so I went outside to check on Aaron. Dinky and Aaron had disappeared. It looked like the rope had been untied from the tree.

I hurried back to tell Mom and Dad, and then we all started searching the neighborhood, calling for Aaron and Dinky as loudly as we could. Once Lola and a few of the other neighbors found out what all the commotion was about, they joined the search. The Talker had been sitting outside the whole time, of course, and Mom actually ran over to ask him if he'd seen anything. He didn't even glance up at her. He just kept talking about dead bodies and Belgian winters.

Mom called the police, and then she and Mrs. Natalie went next door and searched every room in Mrs. Natalie's apartment. Two officers came by, and after they took down all the information they said it shouldn't be hard to spot a dog that big. Lola and I ran down to the schoolyard, but we failed to find so much as a paw print. A few times during the day, I could swear I heard a deep, distant bark, but I could never tell where it was coming from. We crisscrossed the neighborhood all day long, calling and looking and fretting. Mrs. Natalie grew even more frantic, so Grandpa stayed with her at our kitchen table and made her more tea.

Mrs. Natalie was convinced Aaron had run away with Dinky to keep her from sending the dog to the pound. "It's all my fault," she said, again and again. I was convinced that Dinky had simply eaten Aaron and run off to look for more young children with sticky hands.

The two police officers stopped by after dark to check on us. They'd found nothing. Neither had we. Mom and Mrs. Natalie cried again. Dad frowned and tried not to curse. Grandpa cursed freely.

Then, just after a dinner that everyone only picked at, the front door swung open and there stood Aaron. We ran toward him, but he lifted up a hand to stop us. And we stopped. Even Mom stopped. Aaron stood looking at us silently, holding us back with his chubby upraised hand. He tilted his head a bit to one side, whispered something, and waved his hand. Silently and gracefully, Dinky stepped through the door. We could hear her soft panting as she took her place beside Aaron. Aaron tilted his head to the other side. He whispered again and Dinky sat down on her haunches. Another whisper and Dinky lay down. Then Aaron smiled, whispered, and tilted his head again. Dinky stood up, walked quietly to the kitchen—right past all of us and right past Mrs. Natalie. Dinky gently took the refrigerator handle in her mouth and pulled the door open. She stuck her huge head inside. She delicately picked up one of Mom's Diet Pepsi cans, carried it back to Aaron, and lay it at his feet.

"Pretty good, huh?" said Aaron.

Then and only then was Aaron buried in a sea of hugs.

A few minutes later, Aaron pulled Lola and me out of Mrs. Natalie's earshot. Dinky remained lying down, not moving an inch. "It wasn't me who trained Dinky. Not really," said Aaron, quietly. "It was Mr. Daga. When you guys all went inside earlier today, he came out. He was really mad. He said that he wasn't going to let some loudmouthed dog keep him up all night. Either that dog had to learn some manners, or Mr. Daga was going to chase both Dinky and Mrs. Natalie out. Then he invited us inside."

"You took Dinky into Mr. Daga's house?"

"Yup. That's where I've been all day." Aaron explained to us how Mr. Daga had Dinky under control within seconds. Dinky was obeying the rat's commands before they reached the top of the stairs. "Mr. Daga talks Dog."

"He what?"

"He talks Dog. He talks Cat, Rat, and Dog. And English, of course. He learned it all from his dad, he said, who learned it from his dad, who learned it from his, all the way back to Mr. Daga's great-great-great-grandfather. And guess who *he* learned it from?"

"Who?" I said.

"You've got to guess."

"Aaron! Who?"

"Tilton. The guy who owned our house. He learned Rat and taught the rats to learn human English. He did it with something Mr. Daga called amp . . . umm . . . amplified bio . . ."

"Amplified bioacoustics?"

"Yeah."

"Did Mr. Daga teach *you* how to talk Dog?" Lola asked.

"I wish. He said hardly any humans are smart enough to learn it. He called Tilton 'a freak of nature.' It took Mr. Daga all day just to teach me a few basic commands. You have to do them in a really high-pitched voice. So high that most grown-ups can't even hear them."

"Is that what you were doing when you first came in?" I asked.

"Yup. I'll teach you. I can do 'come' and 'sit' and 'lie down' and 'get me a pop from the fridge.' That's all I know. Oh, and Mr. Daga had a long talk with Dinky about bad manners and barking and chewing on things, so she'll be a nice dog for Mrs. Natalie. I think Mr. Daga kind of freaked Dinky out. Mr. Daga's got quite a temper. Now Dinky knows Mr. Daga's the alpha rat."

Mr. Daga's talk worked. Dinky was a different dog from then on: quiet, obedient, and well mannered. Not that it mattered, really. Three days later, she started shrinking.

The shrinking didn't happen the same way as the growing. One day Dinky woke up with her tail shrunk all the way to its original size. It was so much smaller than the rest of her that at first we thought her tail had fallen off. By the next morning her head had shrunk. Her body was still almost pony-sized, but her head was the size of a lapdog's. Her bark was high and tiny again, not that she barked much that day. As a tiny-headed dog, nearly all she did was eat. It took a lot of eating for that tiny mouth to fill that huge belly.

The body shrank next. When Dinky woke up the following morning, she had a tiny dog's body with big dog legs. She looked like a fluffy spider. She kept toppling over so she ended up spending most of the day with her legs sticking out of her doggie bed.

I laughed every time I looked at her. Even Lola laughed. Aaron sat next to Dinky, patting her head and telling her to ignore us.

The next day, Dinky's legs had shrunk and she was back to normal, to the relief of Mrs. Natalie. Actually, she wasn't completely normal. Her right legs had shrunk all the way down, but her left legs stayed just a little bit longer. Most people probably wouldn't have noticed but for the fact that Dinky tended to run in circles.

The one advantage? Whenever Dinky visited our house, she walked perfectly level on our tilting floors, as long as she moved around the house in a clockwise direction.

Mrs. Natalie seemed happy with her obedient little dog, but now that Dinky was so calm, Aaron didn't show much interest in her. Dinky walked softly, almost never jumped, and rarely barked—and Aaron spent less and less time with her. By doing what everyone else wanted, Dinky lost the one thing she wanted the most. Dinky still grew excited when Aaron came around, but now she showed her joy with a quiet wag of her tail. Aaron hardly noticed. I did. So did Lola. "You can see her feelings in her eyes," Lola said. "They look a little sadder than they used to, if you ask me."

But every now and then the two of them—boy and dog—would connect in the old, wild way. It usually happened outside, down by the end of the block, far away from Mr. Daga. Aaron would shout. Dinky would jump. Aaron would tumble. The two of them would roll together in the green summer grass.

THE STORY OF F. T. TILTON

WE'D LOOKED EVERYWHERE for our bikes. The longer we looked for them, the more convinced we became that the Purple Door Man had stashed them in his house.

The sky was clear and blue, but Aaron and I sat in the living room flipping from TV channel to TV channel. Finally, after watching one lousy show after another for about two hours, we grew desperate enough to shut off the TV. We were arguing on the porch about what to do when Lola walked over and stood at the bottom of our front steps. "Who the heck is Tilton anyway?"

"Huh?" I said.

"Tilton," said Lola, gesturing at the sign next to our front door. "Your sign says 'Tilton House.' And Aaron said Tilton taught the Dagas how to speak all those languages. Who is Tilton?"

"I don't know. I guess he's the guy who built this house."

Lola sat next to me. "He must be the one that stayed inside all those years. I wonder if there's some way we could find out more about him," she said.

We'd never found anything that mentioned Tilton other than the sign on the porch.

"Maybe we could look in the attic," Aaron said.

"No way!" I said. "I'm not going back up there."

"I know where we need to look," said Lola, "and so do you. We need to open up that metal box."

"But we've tried a million times," Aaron said.

"What we need is an expert," said Lola. "Someone sneaky."

"We need Mr. Daga," I said suddenly. I couldn't believe I hadn't thought of it before.

"The rat?" asked Lola. "Can I meet him?"

"You *want* to?"

"Yes, Josh Peshik, I want to meet him."

We took Lola with us over to the Dagas' house. We had a routine we went through when we visited them. We'd usually bring a gift of food with us, like a hotdog or a cup of Cheerios. We would knock on the door and then announce ourselves. If they wanted to see us, they would open the door.

This time the door opened and Mr. Daga waved up at us with one paw, absently rubbing his hairless belly with the other. His house smelled so bad, it was hard to breathe. "What's up, little Peshik?" he said. "Is that a hotdog I smell?" I set the hot dog on the floor.

"Who's your lady friend?" asked Mr. Daga.

"This is Lola," I said. "She's our neighbor. She's okay."

"Why's she plugging her nose like that?"

I slapped Lola's hand down and frowned at her. She forced a close-lipped smile and cautiously followed Aaron and me inside.

Since the Dagas had moved in, they'd done a lot of decorating, rat-style. That meant piles: piles of chewed-up toilet paper, piles of chewed-up newspaper, piles of rat poop, and squirming piles of baby rats, all tumbling over one another, looking for something to chew on.

"You sure have a lot of kids, Mr. Daga," said Aaron.

"Tell me about it. Heck, these days I've even got a lot of grandkids. Maybe even some great-grandkids. Who knows? I can barely keep up with all of 'em. Sometimes I think your dad had the right idea, with just the two of you. But Mrs. Daga—she always wanted a big family."

We told Mr. Daga about our problem with the metal box. "Sounds like something I could help you with," he said. His tiny eyes grew bright and his whiskers twitched from side to side. "Let's have a look-see."

We set the box down on the floor. Mr. Daga's little shoulders slumped when he saw it. "Awww, that old thing? Nothing's in there but an old picture and some scribbling."

"You mean you've looked in this box before?"

"Course I have, kid. If it was in your house, I've seen it. That box was up in the attic, right?"

"Yeah."

"I've opened it a bunch of times. Every so often, one of my kids would come across it and think they found something new. They'd always bug me to open it for them. I can unlock it with my eyes closed."

"Could you unlock it for us, Mr. Daga?" asked Lola.

"Sure, but like I said, there's not much in it."

Mr. Daga walked up to the metal box and stuck one of his paws into the keyhole. He reached in all the way to his shoulder, then strained and grunted and grimaced as he pushed and pulled on some unseen gear. Suddenly, we heard a click. Mr. Daga smiled and withdrew his arm.

"There you go, kids. Knock yourselves out. Now if you all will excuse me, I think I hear the wife calling. For all I know, she's busting out a few more babies."

The thought of Mrs. Daga busting out babies chased us out the door and down the stairs. We took the box up to our room and set it on the bottom bunk.

The bottom drawer now slid open easily. Inside, we found an old black-and-white photograph of a woman's face. The corners of the photo were rounded off with tiny bite marks. Mr. Daga and his kids had clearly looked at the photo more than once. The woman in the picture had round, dark eyes, long lashes, and pursed, shiny lips. Her black hair was tied back with a scarf. The photo was signed in a flowing, girlish hand. It said, "Take a piece of my heart" and was signed only with a single letter: *M*.

"She's beautiful," said Lola, her hand going to her hair. "I wonder who she is."

Under the photo lay a thin notebook. When we pulled it out of the drawer, tiny crumbs of paper fell out of it. Its old cover was brown cardboard, colored and textured to give it the look and feel of leather. The word *Journal* was printed across the front. Like the photo, the corners of the book were rounded by tiny teeth marks, and the bottom third of the cover was missing completely. I opened the journal carefully and examined the contents.

The first ten pages were covered with a shakier version of the same slanting, spidery script on the walls of our house. The rest of the book was blank.

"What does it say?" asked Aaron, trying to get a look.

I held the journal away from him.

"Why don't you read it aloud, Peshik?" said Lola.

"Okay, okay. No need to get impatient."

With that, I began to read the following aloud:

I am dying. If not today, then soon. I have no heirs. If you find this book, try to think upon my remains with mercy.

I, Francis Theodore Tilton, was born in 1909, to Henry and Charlene Tilton in Brooklyn, New York. I was a healthy child but for one thing: My left leg was three inches shorter than my right.

My father was a kind and good-natured man and a watch-maker of some renown. I spent many hours at his side, playing with the tiny gears. I made my first working clock when I was seven. My father expressed his pride in my achievement and encouraged my natural abilities.

When I was a boy, Father would create elaborate treasure hunts for me, using the hands of a clock as directional clues. The treasure was always something small—a tool, a carved bit of wood—but the game was a favorite of mine. If you've found this letter, you may be familiar with the game, too.

My mother, a beautiful dark-haired woman with a fiery temper, was my protector and defender. She refused to acknowledge that my uneven legs were a weakness. Thanks to her constant pushing, I excelled in school. I joined the track team and won first place ribbons in the discus and shot put, sports where my shorter leg made it easier to spin my body quickly and powerfully.

Mother taught me to think of my defect as a strength. If my unbalanced gait forced me to watch my step to keep from falling, it also led me to find things on the ground— coins, buttons, old keys. Mother helped me start an extensive coin collection and encouraged my collecting by purchasing rare coins for me.

Do I deny that I was bright? Of course not! I was a genius! I was smarter than any of my classmates and all of my teachers. School was a silly pastime. My childhood friend? Science. I spent my days happily—or at least enthusiastically—in my home, performing electrical and chemical experiments and designing elaborate machinery. Our home was known around our corner of Brooklyn for the mysterious smells that often emanated from it, as well as the occasional explosion. Once I turned our old house cat, Matilda, bright blue with a mixture of oxides. On another occasion I made her disappear entirely by—oh, but that is a tale I have told elsewhere.

All in all, I had a satisfactory childhood. The only trouble I experienced was my own doing, for I had little control

*over my wicked temper. All my life, it's been the cause of
my grief.*

*I recall one incident in particular, when a young ruffian named
Snark made a comment about my crooked posture in front of
a young lady I admired. I waited for Snark after school and
called him out and when he approached*

The rest of this section was missing. The page was badly
chewed by the Dagas. We found a few stray bits that mentioned
something about "broke his nose" and "the local constable." The
story started in again abruptly at the top of the next page.

*and while my mother defended my actions, my father
feared that my fighting at school would come to no good.
He was convinced I'd be better off with an early entry into
adulthood. So in 1926, at the age of seventeen, I entered
into an apprenticeship with Hammersly Shipyards in New
York City. I had little interest in the work. I'd always
pictured myself as a captain of industry or a renowned
scientist. But because of my mechanical aptitude, I reached
the grade of journeyman machinist in less than a year
and then, at eighteen, quit Hammersly to move west,
where opportunity was said to abound. I packed up my
coin collection, my tools, and my few other belongings and
ended up in Tacoma, Washington. It was a bustling port
town and the perfect spot to start my small boat-building
company, Tilton Boats, with a bit of money from my
parents.*

My first commission was for a trawler by a fisherman named

The rest of this page was completely missing, falling under the teeth of the Dagas. We skipped to the top of the next page.

only employee was a skilled carpenter named Lennis. The boat we delivered so far exceeded the expectations of the fisherman that at first the man refused the delivery. He complained that the boat went too fast and that the engine was so quiet that he could not tell when it was running. As far as I know, he never did gain any true appreciation for the craft and for the innovations that filled every square inch of it. When he paid me less than the full amount, I threw the money back in his face and then threw him off the dock into Commencement Bay.

I worked tirelessly, but the rapid success I had imagined eluded me until one day in 1928 when I went into partnership with a tall, thin Swede named Hanson. He had yellow hair and a reputation for good manners and fine clothes. What he lacked in brilliance, he made up for in charm. In our partnership, he smoothed the way for me with our customers, and I created genius work for him. We joined forces because of a shared frustration with a poorly designed bridge that crossed the Thea Foss Waterway in downtown Tacoma. This rigid, street-level railroad bridge kept all ship traffic blocked from the harbor on the seaward side. Hanson and I took it upon ourselves to design a replacement—a kind of drawbridge, which we called the Tilton Tilt-Up. The bridge would tilt up on one side and allow nearly all ships to pass through. This opened the waterway to ship traffic and instantly transformed the Thea Foss Waterway into a bustling center of trade.

On the strength of our bridge design, commissions began to roll in. Despite our youth, Hanson and I became the engineers on numerous projects, from the paving of Pacific Avenue to the Yelm irrigation flume to the installation of the famous totem pole at Fireman's Park. In a matter of four years, Tilton Engineering, as we called our firm, grew into the leading design firm on all of Puget Sound. I had become the captain of industry that had I always imagined.

I confess that at the time, I credited my own genius for our success. Looking back, I can see that Hanson was equally responsible. He was a master administrator, and his firm belief in my abilities pushed us forward. I would never have achieved the level of success on my own that the two of us achieved together. I was abrasive. I know it. Few people liked me. Few ever have. And I've liked even fewer of them.

It was Hanson who taught me how to act like a gentleman. It was he who assisted me in the design of my home, Tilton House, which, for a short time, became something of a landmark in our neighborhood. All the floors slope three degrees toward the center to adjust for the shortness of my left leg. As long as I always travel through the house in a clockwise direction, this slope makes my beloved home the one place where I walk level and where others struggle, unbalanced. Hanson even hired my old employee, Lennis the carpenter, to help with the finishing of the home. Lennis crafted a beautiful porch swing and a dining room set as my first pieces of furniture. I am sitting at the dining room table even now, as I record these facts.

In spite of my abrasive nature, Hanson and I became local celebrities. The two of us were often called upon to meet visiting dignitaries—politicians, movie stars, singers, and the like. We filled that role for a number of years. That was how we met Mary. She was touring the country to promote what was her final film, The Primrose Path, *which ran for two weeks at the Pantages Movie Palace. Hanson and I met her train at Union Station, posed for the local newspaper photographers, and then accompanied her to the Alt Heidelberg, a fine restaurant that had just opened.*

At dinner that night, Mary put forth all of her famous charms. Before we were halfway through the appetizers, she had me wrapped around her little finger. Hanson wasn't far behind. While we were sipping brandy and waiting for dessert, she confessed she was done with Hollywood and had traveled to Tacoma not only to promote her picture, but to find what she called "real love." It may have been the brandy, but I felt as if Mary were speaking to me when she said this.

*At the end of the evening, I pulled Mary aside and asked
her to dinner the following night. She said no, as she had
plans, but that she would love to dine with me the evening
after that. She did. It was glorious. I drove her back to her
room and, on the steps of the Hotel Winthrop, I told her I
was in love with her. "Of course you are," she said, and
kissed me on my lips.*

*Mary left the next morning to continue her promotional
tour. While she was away, she wrote to tell me that*

A few sentences were missing here, chewed away by the rats,
which drove Lola crazy. She said Mary must have told Tilton she
was in love with him, too. The story continued.

*but returned in two months. She stayed at the Winthrop
and I dined with her three or four nights a week—never
more often than that. On many occasions, I tried to ask
her to marry me, but she would put her fingers on my lips
and tell me to shush or would silence me with a kiss. I was
desperate to spend the rest of my life with her. I was madly
in love. Oh, if only I had possessed Hanson's charms.*

*My bliss ended abruptly two months later. A business
acquaintance of mine named Hodgson Bennett shared with
me the devastating news that the rest of Tacoma society
knew already. The reason Mary would see me only three or
four nights a week was because she was spending her other
evenings with Hanson.*

I was overcome. I felt betrayed by the woman I loved and the friend I trusted. My mind turned dark and, I shamefully admit, thoughts of murder filled my head.

That evening, while driving to dinner, I confronted Mary. I told her she had made a fool of me. She apologized and said she did indeed love me, but she loved Hanson as well. At the next stoplight, she opened the car door and stepped out into the shadows. I drove home alone, angry and miserable. I lay awake all night.

In the morning, Mary came to see me at Tilton House. I did not know it then, but it would be the last time I would ever lay eyes on her. She brought a package with her, which she said was something beautiful to remember her by. She had originally purchased it during a trip to

More missing words here.

and many people had remarked how similar they were. She was leaving, she said, because she could not come between Hanson and me. Her final request was that I not hold Hanson responsible for her departure. If I truly loved her, she said, then I would preserve my friendship with Hanson. I hardly heard a word she said. I begged her one last time to become my wife. She refused, kissed me, and left.

I stood on my porch, lost in sorrow, when Hanson showed up, looking for Mary. I told him about her gift, but it failed to bring us together. Forgetting Mary's appeal for peace, the two of us argued heatedly. Hanson struck me in the face. My raging temper, which I had kept in check for so many years, exploded. With all of my might, I struck Hanson back, landing a great blow on the end of his jaw.

Some sentences were mostly chewed away here. The only part we could read said, "didn't know what to do with the body."

That was the end of it. And that was the last I ever saw of him.

In a single, cursed morning, I had lost my best friend and the woman I loved.

I walked away from my business. Indeed, I walked away from all parts of my life. What use was the world, with its fickle women, deceitful friends, and level sidewalks? I decided to turn my face from society and spend the rest of my life with my old childhood friends—engineering, chemistry, electricity, mathematics. So I retreated to my house—this house. Indeed, since that very day, I have never left it. Not once. How long has it been? Six decades? Seven? Perhaps more? I have fully lost track of time.

I am so old now, and so tired. I fear that I will not even finish this page, and I still have so much to tell.

Have I known happiness since that fateful night? No. But I have known great and secret successes. What have I learned? What have I accomplished? The language of beasts is now open to me. I have conversed with the vermin—with the rattus rattus inside my home—and taught them to converse with me. I can turn off the visible with a flick of a switch. Passages through time and space lie within these walls. And I have learned to tap the power of ilex aquifolium, so that the large and the small are interchangeable, albeit not without great risk.

Have I recorded all I know? Yes! But not in books. Not on paper. My house is the document of my achievements. All secrets lie within. And my final revenge is that I hope it takes the world as long to uncover my secrets as it did for me to discover them. To learn them all, you will have to live long.

I am growing wearier than ever. I am so old. My old heart beats weakly. It hurts to breathe.

As for the body—the result of that fateful night—I buried it at six o'clock, in the crawl space under the house. I have no desire to look upon it, as it only brings back bitter memories.

F. T. Tilton

The journal ended there. Aaron, Lola, and I sat in silence.

"Do you know what this means?" Lola finally whispered. "It means you've got a dead body buried in your crawl space! It means you're living in the house of a murderer!"

"I want to go downstairs now," said Aaron in a low whisper.

"But that was only part of it," I said. "It also means that our house holds all kinds of secrets! Talking to animals! Invisibility! And traveling through time and space! He said it's all written on the walls! And besides, that murder happened a long time ago."

"It doesn't matter how long ago it happened," Lola said. "A murderer lived here and the guy he killed is under your house. You're living on top of a murder victim!"

"Shut up, Lola!"

"I want to go downstairs," repeated Aaron.

"Not yet," I said. "First you've got to promise me you won't tell Mom or Dad."

"Why?"

"Because, Aaron, if Mom finds out that someone was murdered in our house and that the dead body is buried in our crawl space, then you know there's no way she'll want to stay here."

"You'd move?" said Lola.

"Mom's barely put up with this place since we moved in," I said. "A dead body would be the last straw—I'm sure of it."

"I don't think I want to stay here, either," whimpered Aaron.

"Oh yes, you do. This is our home and we're staying. There's still too much to discover. So promise you won't tell."

"If I promise, can I go downstairs?"

"Yes."

"Okay. I promise."

"You better not say anything either, Lola."

She glared at me. "Do you actually think I would?"

"No. But don't."

I couldn't eat my dinner that night.

A dead body was buried in our crawl space.

THE MOTHER LODE

I WOKE UP at four the next morning.

The room was dark and still, and my thoughts circled around F. T. Tilton and the murdered man named Hanson who was buried in our crawl space. His body had probably rotted away by now, leaving only the skeleton.

At four thirty, I gave up on sleep. I looked over the side of Aaron's bed. He was curled up in a tight ball and his blanket and sheets had been kicked off. I shuffled downstairs to watch TV. When I reached the entryway, I realized I was probably standing in the same spot where Tilton had murdered Hanson. I glanced around, wondering if there were any bloodstains still hidden in the corners. But there were none that I could see. My eyes fell on the equations: more mysteries when what I wanted were answers.

I walked into the living room and switched on the TV. Nothing was on but infomercials. I watched them anyway. At least they kept me from thinking about the dead body.

Aaron stumbled downstairs around six. He gave me a tired, knowing look. He said he'd had a dream about the body. "It was walking up the stairs to our room. It kept coming closer and closer," he said. "I woke up before it got to me. But just barely. I could feel its breath."

After breakfast, Aaron and I wandered back into the living room and plopped down on the couch. Mom was digging around in her purse for her car keys so she could drive Grandpa across town to a friend's house. "Why are you sitting inside on a day like this?" she wanted to know. "Go ride your bikes or something."

"Can't." I said. "Purple Door Man stole our bikes."

"You don't know that for sure, Josh."

"Yes, I do."

"How?"

"I just know. Everyone knows."

Mom frowned at me. She set down her purse and walked outside to the Purple Door Man's house.

Aaron and I pressed our faces against the front window, but the Purple Door Man's porch was so covered in junk that we couldn't see anything but the top of Mom's head. Only a few minutes went by before Mom came stomping back. She slammed the door after her.

"That—man—is—an—oooh!"

"He's what?" asked Aaron.

116

"Never mind what he is! Do you know what he said to me when I asked about your bikes? He said I should teach my mangy brats some manners! You're not mangy! What a complete—oooh!" She grabbed Grandpa by the arm and nearly dragged him to the car.

After Mom left, I told Aaron we should begin studying the walls to see if we could uncover any of Tilton's instructions for invisibility or time travel. The thought of being able to turn invisible was almost enough to make me forget about the body in the crawl space. Think of the pranks I could pull at school. Think what I could do to the Purple Door Man!

"I don't want to be in the house when Mom's gone," said Aaron. "Can we go outside?"

"Hold on. Look at this," I said as I reread an entryway wall. "Here's Tilton's diagram about amplified bioacoustics. Isn't that what Mr. Daga said Tilton used to learn how to talk to animals?"

"Josh, can we please get out of here?"

So we went outside. We still had no bikes to ride, no balls to kick, and no skateboards to cruise on, but it was good to be outdoors. It's harder to worry about dead bodies when the sun is warming your face.

But not for everybody, I guess. "I can't stop thinking about it," said Lola, who was sitting next to us on the porch steps.

"You don't have to live with it," I said.

"I know. It's creepy." She glanced behind her at our front door, then sighed. "But it's also kind of cool."

"Cool?"

"Yeah. You're the only people I know who live in a murderer's house."

"And?"

"And what? I'm jealous, okay?"

"Okay."

We sat in silence for a few minutes.

"This is stupid," said Lola finally. "I want to do something."

"Like what?"

"I want to ride bikes."

"We don't have any bikes."

"I know. Because the Purple Door Man can't keep his hands off our stuff. That's the stupidest part of the whole thing." Lola paused. "Did you tell your mom and dad yet?" Lola asked.

"Tell them what?"

"You know. About the . . . you know."

"No," I said, "and we're not going to tell them. Can you please stop talking about it?"

Just then a car drove slowly past. The driver had the window down and was looking at something in the Purple Door Man's yard. He parked his car and got out to take a look at the green pickup truck rusting on the grass.

"Owner of this truck live here?" he called to us.

"Yeah," I said.

"Think he'd consider selling it?"

"Probably. He's always buying and selling cars."

A few minutes later, the driver and the Purple Door Man had the hood of the truck open. The Purple Door Man pulled out the old battery from the truck and replaced it with a battery from one of his less junky cars. He climbed inside and turned the key. The truck sputtered and roared to life.

"We can take it for a spin," shouted the Purple Door Man above the roar of the engine. "She runs real smooth on the highway." The prospective buyer climbed in and they drove off.

Lola jumped to her feet. "Now's our chance! Come on!" she yelled.

"Come on where?"

"*Where?* We're getting our bikes back!"

Lola told Aaron to stand out in the street and scream as loud as he could if he saw the truck coming back. She grabbed me and pushed me toward the Purple Door Man's house.

"What are you doing, Lola?" I yelled. "We can't go in there!"

"Shut up, Josh Peshik! I want my bike!" She pushed me up the front steps and we stumbled into the house.

A green canoe hung from the ceiling in the hallway, and car parts lay all over the floor. A pile of umbrellas was precariously propped against a collection of thermoses. Yellowing newspapers leaned in messy stacks from floor to ceiling.

"Hurry," said Lola. We ran into what looked like the living room, where a muted twelve-inch TV glowed among the towering stacks of newspapers. A spot had been cleared on the couch for one person to sit. No bikes here.

We squeezed through tight corridors of newspapers until we reached the kitchen. I wondered how the Purple Door Man and his pumpkin belly could fit through all this stuff. The kitchen was nearly buried in cans of food. Most of the labels were faded and crumbling.

A doorway off the kitchen led to the back of the house. Lola pulled it open.

"I found it!" she cried. "It's the mother lode!"

I followed Lola into the room and saw my bike, right next to Lola's and Aaron's and dozens of others I'd never seen before. And balls, too. Soccer balls, basketballs, footballs, playground balls, and hundreds of baseballs. I could see what looked like my skateboard and helmet under the tangle.

"There's the back door!" said Lola, pointing to a door on the far side of the room. She climbed over the pile of bikes and twisted the knob. The door opened onto the Purple Door Man's backyard. "Hurry! He could come back any minute."

I tried to carry my bike over the mountain of other bikes and balls, but it kept tangling in all the other pedals and spokes.

"Forget it!" cried Lola. "Come over here and help me." I climbed over the pile and we grabbed the bike nearest to the door and pulled it outside.

"Throw it over the fence into your yard!" said Lola.

"Are you serious?"

"Do it!"

Lola and I hefted the bike and tossed it over the shoulder-high fence. It landed on the other side with a crash.

"What was that?" yelled Aaron from the front yard.

"Never mind!" Lola yelled back. "Just keep your eyes peeled!"

We grabbed another bike and hurled it over the fence. Then another and another. We threw the balls over, too. In a few minutes, dozens of bikes and balls lay in a pile in our yard.

"It's the mother lode!" Lola kept yelling.

We finally reached our own bikes and tossed them over the fence. Then we weaved our way as fast as we could through the Purple Door Man's house and out the front door. Aaron was frantically looking up and down the street.

"Any sign of him?" Lola said breathlessly.

"No. Did you get the bikes?"

"Did we ever! Come on!"

We led Aaron through the gate into our backyard to the sprawling pile of balls and bikes.

"What are we going to do with all these?" I asked Lola.

"I don't know," she said, laughing. "If we split them three ways, how many bikes do you think we'd have each?"

Mom drove up just then. There was no way we could hide the pile from her.

"You had no right to enter his home uninvited," she said when we told her. "Then again, I suppose he had no right to take your things."

"He's probably been stealing stuff from kids for years," said Aaron.

"What do you want us to do?" I asked.

After a few seconds she said, "You can keep your own things, but we're donating the rest of it. Now come on. Let's go for a ride." She picked up a girl's bike, checked it for size, climbed on, and shakily rode it into the front yard and onto the sidewalk.

The rest of us climbed onto our bikes and followed my mom. We were riding up and down the sidewalk when the old green pickup pulled to the curb, the Purple Door Man and his potential buyer inside. It took the Purple Door Man only a few seconds to realize we were riding our bikes again. He excused himself to his customer and went quickly inside his house. A moment later, he charged out again. Lola, Aaron, and I stopped riding and watched him nervously.

Only my mom kept riding. She turned wobbly circles in the street, directly in front of the Purple Door Man's house. She greeted the Purple Door Man cheerily. "Nice day for a bike ride, isn't it?" she said.

The Purple Door Man said nothing. He stared at my mom. She smiled back at him. He returned to his house and shut the door. The prospective buyer of the pickup truck waited outside for a while, then walked up to the purple door and knocked, but the man never answered. Finally, the buyer gave up and drove away.

Aaron, Lola, and I rode bikes the rest of the afternoon. Five different bikes each.

THE BLACK SACK

SUMMER WAS ENDING GENTLY, in long, melancholy shadows. Noontimes still felt hot, but by bedtime the house always cooled down. I would have slept well if the murder wasn't weighing so heavily on my mind.

I spent hours each day scanning the walls of our home, and I did move closer to a handful of discoveries. I sat in my room, reading about *ilex aquifolium*. I looked it up in our big unabridged dictionary and learned it was the scientific name for holly—like the holly tree growing in our front yard. But none of the other scribbles in my room made sense to me—at least not yet. It would take a trained scientist years to decipher them all. And if we moved, I'd never learn any of Tilton's secrets. I'd never get to turn invisible.

In the entryway, I studied the diagram labeled "amplified bioacoustics." I looked up *bioacoustics* in our dictionary, which defined it as "the science of animal sounds." If I could make sense out of it, I thought, I could control animals the way Mr. Daga controlled Dinky. Maybe I could make our old cat, Molly, bring me snacks while I lay in bed. I wondered if I could control humans as well.

Behind the couch, I reread "Invisibility, electricity, and the refractive index of air." It was obvious now that it had something to do with the dimmer switch. The wiring diagram next to it must be a wiring system Tilton had experimented with. Dad must have somehow tapped into it.

There was so much here. So much to lose.

I desperately wished I could talk about the murder to someone other than Lola and Aaron. It felt as if the secret would leap out into the open at any time. Whenever Mom or Dad would ask me a question, I would snap an answer back at them, because I felt like they knew I was hiding something.

A week passed and I began to think about the murder and the mysteries less and to focus instead on the few free days of summer we had left. Dad sat Aaron and me down at Jon's Barber Shop and told Jon to get rid of our shaggy summer hair. Mom took us shopping at the mall for back-to-school clothes. I didn't mind because I always liked trying on jeans and sneakers, but I knew that school shopping was the dreaded signal of the end of summer.

Every few days, in the middle of a game or at the end of a long bike ride, my mind always came back to F.T. Tilton's journal and his confession of murder. My stomach would turn and the thought would cast a shadow on the sunniest afternoon.

I wasn't sure which was worse: that we were living on top of the grave of a murdered man, or the possibility that the truth would come to light and we would have to move. I felt certain that if my mom found out about the body, she would insist we sell the house. And who would buy this place? The floors all tilted and the house was a crime scene. Every wall was covered in the scribbles of a murdering mad scientist. Or at least a murdering mad engineer. It didn't matter that he might have the secret of time travel or invisibility written on our walls. We'd still end up back in an apartment. We'd have to leave our beloved Tilton House behind and it would sit empty again. It deserved better. It deserved me, because I loved it. Because I wanted to know its secrets.

The first day of school finally arrived on the Tuesday after Labor Day. I was pacing up and down the front porch, waiting for Aaron, when I spotted something tucked into the branches of the willow tree near the sidewalk.

It was a sack. The top was pulled shut with a coarse drawstring. I tugged it out of the branches. It felt heavy and was made of a sturdy, waxy cloth, mostly black except where it had faded to the color of coffee grounds. Whatever was inside was about the size and shape of a soccer ball.

My fingers moved to the drawstrings and then stopped. What if something horrible lay inside? What if it was connected to another murder? What if a murderer had driven by in the middle of the night and thrown a severed head into our yard? What if I opened the sack, found the head, and then turned it over to the police? They would question me. I'd tell them how I'd found it stuck in the branches of a tree in my front yard. They wouldn't believe me. After all, how many people find a head in their front yard? After weeks of investigation, they still wouldn't have any other suspects, so they'd put me in jail. I'd die in the electric chair before my thirteenth birthday.

On the other hand, what if the sack was filled with a chunk of gold? Or jewels? What if opening it made me rich? If I put it back in the tree, someone else would find it. They'd open it and get rich instead of me.

And what if it was somehow connected to Tilton, to our house, and to the body in the crawl space?

I knew Mom and Aaron would step out the front door any second, so I stashed the sack behind a bush next to our front porch without looking inside. As soon as I had hidden it, the front door opened. I jumped at least six inches.

Mom hustled Aaron and me into our van. "Are you excited?" she asked.

"W-what?" I sputtered. "What do you mean?"

"It's a simple question, Josh. Is something wrong?"

"No!"

"I just asked if you were excited. About school. Obviously you are. Or maybe you're a tad bit nervous. It's okay to be nervous."

I was nervous, all right, but not about school. Usually the first day of school was one of the big days of the year, but I barely remember anything about that day other than the black sack.

At the end of the school day, I met Aaron and Lola outside of Tilton House and showed them the sack. Lola immediately grabbed it, pulled the string, and opened the top. She screamed. Then she looked again, made a face, and laughed with embarrassment.

"I thought it was real," she said.

I looked in. A head looked back at us. It was made of stone. I pulled it out. It was the head from the statue of a beautiful woman. Her eyes reminded me of the way Aaron's eyes look when Mom catches him stealing a cookie or watching TV when he's not supposed to—guilty and innocent, both at the same time. He looks guilty because he did something wrong, but at eight years old, innocence is still part of the package.

When Dad came home from the museum, we showed the head to him and Mom. Dad's jaw dropped open.

"You found this in the front yard? In *our* yard? So it's ours? It's very old. It looks Greek—or maybe an Italian Renaissance reproduction of Greek. The museum will probably flip over this, Josh. Would you mind if I took it down and showed it to them?"

I didn't mind. I asked if I could come along and Dad said yes.

The next day, Dad picked me up from middle school in his pickup and drove us back to the museum. The black sack lay on the seat between us.

When we reached the museum, Dad led me into a long room full of grown-ups. I recognized the red-faced man at the end of the table as Mr. Stevens, Dad's boss—the same guy who had gotten mad at Dad about the dimmer switch.

"So this is the boy, eh, Hal?" said Mr. Stevens. He turned to me. "It's Josh, right?"

"Yes. Hello."

"Why, hello to you, too, Josh. My name is Mr. Stevens." He was talking to me in a slow, syrupy voice, as if I were a little kid.

"I know."

"You do? You're a smart boy, Josh. Did you also know I'm your dad's boss?"

"Yes."

"I'm the director of this whole museum. I understand you may have found something pretty special."

"I guess so," I said.

"Can we see what you found, Josh?"

My dad carefully set the sack in the middle of the table. He pulled out the head. Mr. Stevens's face grew redder than ever. The room immediately went into an uproar.

A week went by before the story hit the newspaper. It took the people at the museum that long to figure out that the head belonged to an important Italian statue that had disappeared from the collection of a rich American woman before World War II. The statue was of a woman called Pandora and was made by an Italian guy named Benvenuto Cellini in the fifteen hundreds. The newspaper ran an old black-and-white photograph of the statue, which showed the head attached to a smooth white body. One of the statue's hands was outstretched, and the other grasped a partially opened box. A single, tiny, fairylike creature was flying out of that box.

Dad told me that Pandora was a character from an old Greek myth—she was a mortal who was given a box full of all the sins and sorrows of the world. When Pandora broke the rules and opened it, all the sins and sorrows flew out and poisoned the world with pain and death, fear and hate. The last thing that flew out of the box was hope, which had never existed until that moment. Now that I knew the story, I understood why Pandora's face looked guilty and innocent at the same time.

Mr. Stevens was very excited, Dad said, and was constantly thanking Dad for bringing the head of Pandora to them. "Stevens told me this was going to put the museum on the map," he said at dinner one night. "And he said my contribution is sure to be rewarded."

"Rewarded? What does that mean, 'rewarded'?" asked Mom. "And don't you mean *Josh's* contribution?"

"Sure. Yeah. What I meant was that we found it in our yard—"

"*Josh* found it, you mean."

"Right. And we didn't try to sell it to a big East Coast museum. We kept it here in Tacoma, so I'll be rewarded. I'm thinking promotion, raise, bonus. And I'm thinking soon."

"Soon would be good," said Mom. "We could sure use the money."

I was doing some thinking of my own. I was thinking that maybe if Dad got a big promotion, Mom would be so happy that she'd let us stay in our house, dead body and all. I began to plan just what I would say to her. I'd tell her that if we hadn't moved into this house, we never would have found the sack and Dad never would have gotten his great new job.

Things looked even better the next day when the story hit the local newspaper. The first article actually made the front page. The next day the story ran in newspapers all over the country, and our phone was ringing off the hook. Stevens and the rest of the folks at the museum had never been happier. "Now *this* is the kind of publicity the museum needs, Hal," said Mr. Stevens to Dad.

Then a different article hit the local paper, by the reporter named Van Leopold. It focused on the strange coincidence that a lost work of art this important should be found in the yard of an art museum employee. Van Leopold recalled that great works have been uncovered before, in the attics of widows and plumbers and the like, but never in the yard of someone who actually worked for an art museum. What were the chances? Wasn't it more likely that this employee, Hal Peshik, was involved in something shady and was using his mysteriously ill-gotten gains to forward his own career? After all, said the article, wasn't this the same Hal Peshik who had made the absurd claim that his house temporarily disappeared?

Dad threw the paper in the trash. He fired off a letter to the editor, which the newspaper printed a few days later, but by that time other papers around the country were running versions of Van Leopold's article, all of which pointed a suspicious finger at Dad.

A few days later, Dad came home from work three hours early. "Unpaid leave of absence," he explained, which basically meant he'd been fired. Stevens had told him the museum couldn't risk a scandal and had to distance themselves from Dad and the discovery of Pandora's head.

"Can they do that?" asked Mom.

"I don't know," said Dad. "I'm calling Cal Landgren."

Dad had known Cal Landgren since college. He was a lawyer. Later that night, Cal sat with Dad and Mom around the kitchen table. Cal was tall, thin, and always wore tiny rectangular glasses and a suit so dark blue that it was almost black.

"As far as your job, they can do pretty much whatever they want," said Cal. "You don't have a contract with them. You have what is called 'at-will employment,' which means they can fire you for any reason at all."

"What about the head?" said Mom. "They can't take it, can they? After all, Josh is the one who found it."

"Well, technically, Josh found it on city property, since it was less than ten feet from the street. That means the city and the museum can keep it unless its rightful owner shows up. If it had been in your house or at least farther away from the street, that would be a different matter."

Dad said, "Stevens had the gall to tell me I might find it a con-solation to know the head of Pandora will hold a place of honor in their permanent collection. What a rat!"

"That's an insult to rats. Mr. Daga is a rat," corrected Mom. "Stevens is a fink. So what do we do now?"

Dad smiled weakly. "I say we look on the bright side. This could be just the break I need. I've been meaning to try my hand at writing again. I'll pull out my old typewriter and get started on a couple of stories. We'll try to keep paying the bills until this thing blows over. And hopefully I can return to work by the end of the month."

It didn't blow over. September ended and Dad spent less and less time writing and more time filling out applications and send-ing out resumes. By the end of October, we'd spent nearly all of our savings and Dad had still not found another job. The stack of unpaid bills on the kitchen counter was growing higher and higher. Mom expanded her part-time job in the school office to as many hours as she could get, but it didn't pay much. I knew times were hard when Grandpa started asking Mom to buy him the cheapest tobacco she could find when she went to the store.

A week before Thanksgiving, Dad called a family meeting and all of us gathered in the living room. "Boys, Dad," he said quietly, "if you remember when we moved into this place, we could barely afford the payments. That was when I was working. Now I've been out of work for almost three months. The money coming in from Mom's job and my unemployment checks isn't enough to keep us living here."

"Maybe I could get a job, too," said Grandpa.

"Dad, you're already giving us most of your Social Security. I don't even like taking that. The fact is that if I can't find a job by the beginning of December, then we will need to sell the house and move back into an apartment."

"Sell Tilton House?" I said. "You can't!"

"It looks like we'll have to, Josh."

"Maybe we could just dim it," Aaron said. "We could use the dimmer switch to make the house disappear and then no one would know we were still here. We could stay forever."

Dad smiled grimly. "I wish it were that easy, pal. But it won't work. If I don't find a job soon, we're sunk."

THE TALKER

DESPAIR. I knew from a recent vocabulary test that *despair* meant "to lose all hope." I'd just lost all of mine, so the definition fit.

My parents sat in our living room, talking about moving as if it were no big deal. All the kids in my class lived in houses, but my parents couldn't keep our house—not even an old house like Tilton House with tilting floors. I bet no one else in my class would even be willing to live in this weird, old house. I'd been worried we'd lose it because it hid the body of a murdered man, but now we were going to lose it because of Dad's stupid job.

"What is wrong with you people?" I shouted at Mom and Dad. "Why can't you even give us a decent place to live?"

I didn't wait for an answer. I jumped up and ran outside into the night. It was late November. Fog sat low and cold on the ground, and I was wearing only a T-shirt and jeans. My feet were bare, and the cold ground hurt with every step. I shivered and instantly wished I could go back in, but my pride and my despair kept my bare feet moving forward. I walked into the fog, which was growing so thick, it made all the familiar neighborhood land-marks look blurry and spooky.

I walked down an uncounted number of streets, making no attempt to keep my tears and anger in check. The fog made the streetlights useless. Instead of illuminating the ground, the light hovered high above. The sidewalk was shrouded in the mist and dark.

I made a few turns and assumed I was walking back in the general direction of my house, but I recognized nothing. I might have even passed Tilton House and not known it. Then I heard a voice in the mist and knew I'd wandered back to my own block. It was the voice of the Talker, and he was chattering about war again. His mumbles guided me like a crazy foghorn.

"Three combat units made up the 187th Division," said the Talker. "Each unit included a regiment of artillery and a regiment of infantry."

"Hi," I called dejectedly as he came into view.

"The 187th fought against established German positions, against much larger numbers," the Talker replied. "It was the heart of winter, December and January, and we never received our heavy boots."

"My dad lost his job," I said, sitting down on the steps next to him, "and it looks like we're going to have to sell our house."

"The Germans were holed up in each town, while we had

to attack from snow-covered open ground, without our heavy boots," he responded.

"I don't want to move," I said. "I love our house. I love its secrets. I love this neighborhood, even though the Purple Door Man is a complete jerk. I even like you, and you're nutty as a fruitcake."

"Each day, we suffered heavy losses," he went on. "My feet and the feet of my men were so cold, they were numb. Men lost toes to frostbite. Some lost so many they were unable to walk. We searched the German bodies for decent boots, but found theirs were worse than ours. I was the oldest field officer of the 187th. My soldiers were more boys than men. Even though the odds were against us, even though these boys were the youngest division of World War II, the 187th refused to yield."

"Are you trying to tell me something?" I said.

"I can recall sitting for hours, waiting for commands and watching as truckloads of cold, dead bodies were hauled from the battlefield."

"Gross. Can't you talk about something else?"

The Talker paused for a few seconds, then said, "It was the movie *The Shopgirl,* in 1927, which was to define her career." I wondered if his change of topic was coincidence or if he was responding to my request.

"I wish I could do something," I said, mostly to myself. "To save our house, I mean."

"At the height of her popularity she received more than forty-five thousand fan letters a month," the Talker said. "Her last film was in 1933. It was called *The Primrose Path.*"

"That sounds familiar," I said, trying to remember where I'd heard that movie title before.

"On the last night I saw her, she gave Francis and me a beautiful treasure."

"Treasure? That's what I need right now."

"I ended up with only a small part of it. The rest is likely buried. Under fourteen eighteen."

"Under what?" I said. "Did you say fourteen eighteen? That's my address! That's the address of Tilton House! What kind of treasure?"

But the Talker's ramblings had returned to the war and the struggles of the 187th again. It didn't matter. I'd heard enough.

BODY AND SOUL

I RAN ACROSS THE STREET and back into the living room, where
Mom, Dad, Aaron, and Grandpa were still sitting around the
coffee table. I began telling them, as fast as I could, what the
Talker had said about treasure being buried under 1418 and
how 1418 was our house number and how all we had to do was
dig under our house and we'd be rich and we wouldn't have to
move.

"Who told you this, Josh?" asked Dad, tiredly.

"The Talker, Dad! He said some actress gave him and Francis
a beautiful treasure and he'd only gotten part of it and the rest
was buried under fourteen eighteen."

"Francis? Who's Francis? What are you saying, Josh? You think we should dig around under our house for buried treasure?"

"Yes!"

"It's a lovely thought," he said as he got to his feet. "A lovely dream from a crazy man. Maybe I'll dream about it tonight. I'm going to bed." He walked out of the kitchen. Mom smiled at me sadly and joined him.

I sat in silence with Grandpa and Aaron for a few minutes. Finally, Grandpa said, "So the crazy old guy really said all that?"

"He did!" I replied, exasperated.

"And who exactly is Francis?"

"Francis Tilton. As in *Tilton* House."

"Well then," said Grandpa, "we may as well start. Lead the way, Josh."

We managed to scrounge up a few flashlights that actually worked, and grabbed a couple of shovels from the garage. Grandpa grunted and creaked through the little door into the crawl space under the house. The low ceiling forced him to hunch down. He found the light switch and clicked it on. The lone light-bulb gave off a dim glow—just enough to illuminate the hundreds of cobwebs.

"It's a mighty big space," said Grandpa. "If we have to dig up the whole underside of the house, we'll be here till I die."

Then it hit me. In my excitement to find buried treasure, I was standing in the dark, ready to dig under the house, and I'd completely forgotten about what F. T. Tilton had said in his journal. I'd forgotten about the body that was possibly, at this very moment, beneath my feet.

My voice shook as I told Grandpa about the journal and the body. "We should get out of here," I said.

Grandpa squinted into the darkness and then turned to face us. "If you boys don't mind, I think I'm going to light my pipe and have me a smoke. I always think better when I smoke." Aaron and I watched as Grandpa struck a match on an overhead beam and lit his bowl of tobacco. It glowed red like hot coal. Grandpa put away his matches and stared at us through the smoke.

"Now, if I was to bury a treasure down here," he said, "where would I do it? Or where wouldn't I do it? I wouldn't put it by any pipes that went underground, 'cause if one of them busted and somebody had to dig it up, I wouldn't want 'em finding my treasure. So we don't have to dig where any of the pipes are buried. That should take out a good chunk of the space."

"But what if we find the body, Grandpa?" I asked.

"Josh," Grandpa said, as he stared at his pipe, "good things don't come easy. Look at your parents, for instance. Look how hard it's been for them to get this home for you boys. Taken 'em years. You can't expect to just look beneath your house and find a pile of gold laid out for you. You got to take a risk, one way or another. You find either something good, or something bad. But at least you find something. Now then, we can dig, or we can run away like babies. What's it gonna be?"

"What about Mom? If we find a dead body, do you think she'd keep living here?"

"Your mother? She's one of the strongest, wisest women I've ever known. A pile of old bones isn't going to bother her. Don't you worry about your mom. Now, what's it gonna be?"

Aaron and I looked at each other.

"What's it gonna be?" Grandpa repeated.

"Dig," Aaron said.

Who was I to wimp out on my eight-year-old brother? "Dig," I repeated.

"Fine, boys. Where do we start?"

"Maybe he buried it by the chimney," said Aaron.

"Maybe," said Grandpa. "Maybe so." He hobbled toward the furnace chimney, where a column of brick stood in the dirt. Before he'd reached the spot, his wooden leg slipped out from under him and he landed on the ground with a thud. Grandpa let loose with a long string of beautiful curse words, so big and bold, I could swear they almost lit up the darkness.

"Sorry about that, boys," he finally said, lying flat on his back, "but by the time you reach my age, you learn to save the four-letter words for special occasions. Now come on over here and help me to my feet."

We scrambled over and pulled him up. Aaron found Grandpa's pipe and handed it to him. Grandpa wiped it on his sleeve and set about repacking it with fresh tobacco. He fished another match from his pouch and struck it on the beam above his head. The flare of the match lit up the dark, casting weird shadows on Grandpa's upturned face.

Grandpa kept looking up and when the match went out, he lit another. "Look here, boys," he said. The flame illuminated the words "six o'clock" in white chalk.

"Six o'clock!" I shouted. "I know what that means! Six o'clock points straight down!" I explained to Grandpa about the words I'd found in the attic.

Grandpa grunted. "Straight down is right where I'm standing. We may as well give 'er a shot."

Aaron and I started digging directly under the white words. Aaron's shovel kept clanging against mine, and I couldn't seem to get much dirt into each scoop. After fifteen sweaty minutes, we'd barely scratched the surface and Grandpa's patience had run dry.

"No offense, boys, but you stink at this. Kindly step aside and let a one-legged old man show you how it's done." Grandpa grabbed a shovel and stabbed it deep into the dry ground. In less than a minute, he'd dug more than Aaron and I had in fifteen.

Half an hour later Grandpa's hole was four feet deep. Then his shovel hit something hard. We shone our flashlights into the hole and saw white peeking from beneath the dirt. Grandpa climbed out and had me go down into the hole. I began to brush away the dirt from around the object.

Aaron screamed. It was a hand. A white hand. We hadn't found the treasure. We'd found the body instead.

I scrambled out of the hole and Aaron clutched Grandpa's shirt so hard, he almost pulled them both to the ground.

"Settle down now, boys. It ain't alive. Aaron, quit tugging on me. Hold the light still and shine it down there so I can see it." Aaron managed to obey, and Grandpa squinted into the hole. "I can't see from here. Josh, get back down there and clean off more of the dirt."

I thought I was going to throw up. "You want me to go down there?"

"You heard me. Don't take all night."

I took a breath and carefully lowered myself into the hole. With the toe of my shoe, I kicked away at the dirt, ready for the hand to reach out and grab me at any moment. The hand didn't move. I knelt down and scooped away some dirt. The hand was attached to a smooth white arm.

It took us another hour of slow and careful digging to uncover the whole secret. The arm was attached to a body, and the whole body appeared to be made of hard white marble. We'd found the statue of a woman in wonderful condition—except that it was missing its head. It was Pandora.

When we uncovered Pandora's other hand, it was holding a partly opened box, just as the newspaper articles described. A single tiny figure, like a fairy, was flying out of the box. That would have been hope, I guessed.

Tucked inside the box lay something else—a rolled-up leather pouch. Grandpa opened the pouch and carefully pulled out a moldy sheet of paper. It was a letter addressed to Francis Theodore Tilton.

"Who's it from?" I asked.

"I'll be," said Grandpa, staring at the fragile paper intently.

"*What?*" Aaron and I cried.

"It's from Mary Preston."

"Who's Mary Preston?"

"Mary Preston was a movie star. Way back in the early days of the talkies—the first talking pictures. She was a real beauty. 'The beautiful shopgirl,' they called her."

"Mary!" I said. "That must be the Mary that Tilton wrote about in his journal. What's the letter say?"

In the dirt and the dark, next to the white, headless body, Grandpa read the letter aloud:

Dearest Francis,

I traveled to your beautiful Tacoma looking for happiness. It appears I've somehow managed to bring misery with me.

You were so kind to me. I loved you in my own untidy way. But I loved Hanson, too, and that could never work.

142

If I found I was the cause of the end of your friendship with Hanson, I would never be able to forgive myself. Please don't let things end this way. I am leaving, but I am giving both of you a single gift. This statue is my most prized possession, and I want you and Hanson to have it. Let it keep you together. May you share fond memories of me.

With love,
Mary Preston

We pieced together what must have happened. After Mary had left the statue and said goodbye to Tilton, Hanson had come over to Tilton House. The two had fought over the statue and it had somehow broken. Tilton had buried the body in the crawl space so Hanson wouldn't find it, and Hanson, assuming he had survived his fight with Tilton, must have taken the head. No one had been murdered. The body and the treasure were one and the same.

But who was Hanson? How and why did Hanson or someone else leave the head in front of our house? And how did the Talker know the body of the statue was buried under 1418?

"Grandpa, do you know the Talker's real name?"

"I don't. That's all we've ever called him."

"Come on," I said. "We're going to dig through his garbage."

THE NAME ON THE SIGN

THE LIGHTS WERE OFF in our parents' bedroom. I led Grandpa and Josh across the street and into the alley behind the Talker's house. We found the green garbage can against his back fence and opened it. It stunk like rotten vegetables. I started pawing through it without hesitation.

"We just need to find a piece of mail—an envelope or a bill or anything. Here's one!" I pulled out a crumpled envelope from the gas company and unfolded it under the glare of my flashlight. The name on the envelope was Karl Hanson. The Talker was Hanson.

Josh and I ran home as Grandpa clunked quickly behind us. The front door was locked for the night. We pounded on it with our fists until Mom and Dad woke up and flung it open. We spilled the whole story there on the porch. Then we led Mom and Dad down to the crawl space to take a look at the statue. Dad whistled low when he saw it. "Well, Josh," he said, "you may not have found buried treasure, but I think you got my job back."

It turned out we got much more than that.

We skipped school the next morning. After breakfast, I looked outside. The Talker—Karl Hanson—had already taken his regular place on his front steps. He was babbling away again about the 187th when Dad and I lined our wheelbarrow with blankets and rolled Pandora over to his house. For the first time since we moved in, the Talker stopped talking. He looked at the headless statue, smiled softly, and said, "Dora." We set Dora on his porch, and Hanson stared up at it in silence.

Dad called Cal Landgren, his lawyer friend, and told him about the letter and how it proved Karl Hanson's ownership of the statue. It took another couple of days, but Cal brought a court order down to the museum and returned to our house with Pandora's head packed in a wooden crate.

"It's nice to have the head back," said Mom, "but what about Hal's job? We've got bills to pay, you know."

"All in good time, my dear lady," said Cal with a smile.

"First, we need to bring Dora's head back to her body," said Dad.

Dad and I walked over to Karl Hanson's house. It was raining, so Karl was sitting inside on a comfortable chair. He stopped talking and smiled when he saw us through his front window. We took that for an invitation and stepped inside.

"We have something for you, Karl," said Dad. He pulled the head carefully from the wooden crate and handed it to him. Karl

146

smiled at the head as he took it from Dad. He carried it out onto the porch and set it carefully on Dora's body. It fit perfectly. The crack circled Dora's neck like a silver chain.

Karl turned back to Dad and said, "Mary gave her to me. I loved Mary."

"I know you did," said Dad. "She loved you, too, Karl."

Karl took Dad's hand and set it on Dora's arm. "You have her," he said to Dad. "You're young enough to love her. I'm too old."

Dad found out it was impossible to argue with the Talker, so the next day Cal Landgren drew up papers giving Dad complete and legal ownership of the head and body of Pandora. Dad and Cal went back to the museum for what Dad called "an important meeting." This turned into another meeting and then a whole series of meetings that lasted weeks. The first of December came and went, but I heard nothing more about us moving.

During that time, the newspaper found out what had happened and Van Leopold, the reporter, wrote a series of stories, which got picked up again by papers all over the country. This time, all of us—Dad and Grandpa and Aaron and I—came out looking like heroes.

Dad called the family into the living room and finally explained what all the meetings had been about. The museum wanted Dora. They knew Dora was the source of all their publicity and their rise in attendance. They also knew Dad owned her free and clear. Dad wanted the museum to have her, too, but he also knew the statue was really valuable. In their last meeting, both sides had finally agreed on a price for the statue. "Two point three million dollars," Dad said. "With all the publicity, they said it would be well worth it. I could have gotten twice that at the bigger museums back east, but I want her to stay in Tacoma."

147

The museum offered Dad his job back, but he said no. "I was as polite to that fink Stevens as I could stand to be," he said, "since the museum is paying so much for Dora."

"If you're not going to work there, what are you going to do?" I asked.

"Stay home," Dad said. "I like hanging around this old house, tilting floors and all. I may finally get around to photographing these walls. And I may finally get around to writing."

"What would you write?" I asked.

"Your grandpa's not the only one who's got stories to tell. Heck, I might even write a few stories about this strange old house. Oh, and Josh," Dad said, in his low, serious tone, "we have you to thank for all of this—you and Aaron and Grandpa. Don't think I don't know it. Your mother and I are setting aside a good chunk of money for you and your brother in a trust fund. But we both agree you deserve something now. Something significant." Dad mentioned an amount of money he said I could spend as I wanted. I'm not going to say how much it was, but Grandpa used the same amount to buy a brand-new Cadillac. It was not black.

No one asked us to, but Aaron and I shared enough of our money with Lola to make her smile.

"So you're staying?" Lola asked.

"We're staying," I said.

"Good. Because I like having you around here, Peshik."

"I like having you around here, too, Dolores." She punched me. She kept punching until I promised never to call her Dolores again.

The Talker still sat out on his steps, talking away, on sunny days and still sat inside, talking away, when it rained. I never completely figured out his life story, but Grandpa and Dad and I have what we think is a pretty good guess:

We know the Talker, Karl Hanson, was Tilton's partner when they met Mary. Tilton's journal said Mary was promoting her last movie, *The Primrose Path*, which we found out was released in 1933. That must have been when Tilton and Karl had their final fight. Karl did talk about Mary every now and then, but mostly he talked about the 187th. Grandpa had friends who had fought in World War II. He called some of his buddies, and one of them remembered the 187th as the division that fought at the Battle of the Bulge, one of the bloodiest battles in the whole war. Almost 100,000 German soldiers and 20,000 American soldiers died there.

Dad guessed that after Mary left, Karl went off and joined the army and he was still in the army when the war started eight years later. "Surviving something like the Bulge couldn't have been easy," Dad said. "Considering everything that Karl's probably been through, it's a wonder he's not crazier."

One night we brought Karl over to our house for dinner, but it turned into a complete disaster. Mom tried to act as if he were a normal dinner guest, but the guy never shut up, even for a second. It's hard to eat when a crazy old guy with a mouth full of peas is talking about all the dead bodies he's seen.

Sometimes Grandpa hobbles over and sits next to Karl to smoke his pipe. He says that every so often Karl will pause to take a breath and look over at him and smile. Grandpa figures that means he likes the company.

Soon after all the commotion, Aaron, Lola, and I went to visit Mr. Daga to tell him what had happened.

"You mean that old headless statue was worth money? You humans think the strangest things are valuable."

"You knew it was there?"

"Of course, I did, young Peshik. I know everything there is to know about that old house of yours. Haven't I told you that?"

"Everything?" I asked.

"Well, almost everything." That was all he would say.

The Purple Door Man still yelled at us, but at least he stopped stealing our bikes. One day Lola accidentally left her bike in front of our house all through dinner, and when she went outside, it was still there.

Even with Dinky around, Mrs. Natalie seemed lonely. Once she mentioned hearing strange sounds in her kitchen during the night. "I wonder if Mr. Natalie's ghost is fixing himself a sandwich," she said to Dad. It was probably only Mr. Daga or one of his children raiding her garbage.

Sometimes when Aaron and I work in her garden, Mrs. Natalie talks about how alone she is now that Mr. Natalie is gone, but she seems to accept this with one of those grim smiles that belong only to old people. She does have one thing to cheer her up—she and Grandpa started going out for dinner once a week a few months ago. Now it's up to twice a week. He drives, because his new Cadillac is an automatic and works fine with his wooden leg.

All the writing on the wall? I'm dedicated to figuring it out. I've compiled a stack of notebooks, broken down by subject. So far, I haven't made sense out of anything, but I'm sure a breakthrough is not far off. And so far, Dad's still managed to avoid painting over any of it. He still hasn't photographed it yet, either, but he says it's on his to-do list.

One last thing: We still have that sign next to the front door that says TILTON HOUSE. After he sold the statue and paid off our home loan, Dad added a little brass plaque right below it.

The plaque says HOME OF THE PESHIK FAMILY.

ACKNOWLEDGMENTS

THANKS TO MY brilliant and patient editor, Abigail Samoun, for turning my pages of squishiness into a tight story. Abi, I only have one request: Could you be right a little less often? Thanks to my high school English teacher from a million years ago, Glenna Frederick, for making me love writing, even if she did force me to listen to Simon and Garfunkel records. Thanks to the teachers and students at Washington-Hoyt Elementary School for reading my manuscript and saying nice things. Go Cougars! And a special thanks to my kids—Ben, Abel, Bizayehu, and Genet—for asking me to tell them stories and then actually listening.